Private Eye Murders

By Bob Moats

For information and address:
Magic 1 Productions
P.O. Box 524, Fraser MI 48026-0524
Website: http://murdernovels.com
Cover by Bob Moats

Extra special thanks to:

Special thanks to Susan Haughton, who edited this book and for her great suggestions.

Thanks to the beta readers Cindy Valstad, Al Norris, Carolyn Linington, Fleur Wilkinson, Amy Morningstar, and Patrick Barry.

Thank you to all the people who purchased this book. I hope you enjoy it as much as I enjoyed writing it for my faithful readers.

The Jim Richards Family of Readers is listed in the back of the book.

Private Eye Murders

Chapter 1

I was relaxing in my office, as my toy Yorkie, Willy, was snoozing on my desk, when Lacey came storming in.

"Got another good reason for you to be out of town," she said with glee. "This just came in the mail for the office."

She handed me the brochure that had blazed in big letters on the cover, "Premier Private Investigator Conference" and I saw it was being held in Detroit. It had been many months since Penny and I were back in Michigan. I unfolded the brochure and read, as Lacey stood there.

"Do you have something else to say?" I asked her.

"I'm just waiting to hear you say that you're going," she replied with a grin.

"You love any excuse to get me to leave my office and even Las Vegas. You signed me up for that book convention out in New York, and you were happy when Penny and I went back to Michigan for our high school reunion."

"Don't forget the book tour you and Penny went on around the country. I really enjoyed the quiet of the building back then."

"I don't make that much noise, do I?"

"It's not so much the noise, as it's the wandering around you do in the office, looking for something to do. You stopped going out on cases ever since we got Deacon on the staff. With Lynn, Earl, Trapper, and Buck now a detective, you have nothing to do."

"I felt like retiring a little. Have more time to do the things I enjoy."

"Like bugging me," Lacey said with a grin. "Honestly Jim, I love you like a father, but I don't want my father looking over my shoulder while I work."

"So noted. I'll leave you alone more often. Now go out so I can read this," I said unfolding the brochure more. "Have you told any of the others about this?"

"Nope, it just came in and I wanted you to see it first."

"Thank you for thinking of me first. If you see Deacon, ask him come in here."

She said she would, and left my office. I read the brochure about the first private investigator convention that was going to be held at the MGM Grand Hotel and Casino in Detroit. Great, I thought, I'd be leaving Las Vegas with all its hotels and casinos, and going back home to another hotel casino. I could visit my family while out there. I haven't seen my mother in a while, although I do call her every week. If I missed a week, she would call me to scold.

It was a nice brochure, full color with lots of photos of the hotel and the casino. Since it was the first convention, they didn't have any pictures of private eyes running around. I wondered who was in charge of the festivities and organizing the whole thing. I know there were a dozen or so investigating firms in the Southeast Michigan area. When I shut down my office back there to move to Vegas, it was one less.

I heard someone coming down the hall and watched the door. It was Deacon. He was grinning as he came in and plopped down in my client chair. I remember when I first met the gentle giant. It was when Penny was being threatened by the killer of our classmates back home. As a cop, he was assigned to help guard her, and he stuck to us through all the danger and chases.

"What's up, Boss?" he said.

I handed him the brochure and said, "There's a convention of P.I.s back home, and I thought of you. I'm going to mention it to Trapper and Earl since they both came out here with us from Michigan. Lynn may enjoy going, also. May as well take the whole firm, just for the experience.

He was glancing at the features of the convention. "They'll have demonstrations of new surveillance equipment that I'd like to see. And lectures by high profile P.I.s, which will be good.

Have you told Penny about it yet?" Deacon asked.

"Nope, haven't seen her yet. She's still taping her talk show, but she should be in soon. She didn't have any family in the Detroit area, but she might like to visit the house she left, but still owns. My son and his family are living in it, now."

"Well, I'm all for it. We can visit our families while there. Trapper's mother is still there and Buck has family, doesn't he? A brother I think."

"Yep, and more. He had a big family as I remember. If you see Trapper or Earl, have them see me. Do you have a case that you're working on?" I asked, taking back the brochure.

"I talked to a woman who had her jewelry stolen in the hotel where she was staying. She doesn't think the police took an active interest in the case. So she found us and hired me. I'll be out the rest of the day talking to the Excalibur Hotel security."

"Be nice to them, they don't mind working with us, and we need to keep them happy. Where's Lynn?"

"Home with little Penny and nursing her back to health. Damn flu is hitting everyone. Lynn's concerned that she'll be all right."

"I hope she gets better. Go do your thing, and I'll go hunt up the rest of the crew and tell them about this convention."

We both stood, and I picked up Willy from my desk. He was watching us talk, and I put him on the floor. He shot out of the office and headed to the front. Probably to visit with Lacey. Deacon went to his office as I headed back to where Trapper and Earl had their offices. I knew Buck was out, so I passed by his door.

As I was coming up to Trapper's office, I was nearly knocked over by Fred, our handyman, coming out of his room.

"Sorry, Jim, I was in a rush," he said smiling.

"That's okay. Where are you off to?" I asked.

"There's a sale on plants and flowers at a local nursery. I need to fill in the garden out back where some of the foliage died."

"Your flower garden always amazes me. Keep up the good work, Fred. Where's your puppy, Henry?"

"He's in the dog run, I'm going to take him with me," Fred answered.

"Good. Have you seen Trapper or Earl?" I asked.

"Haven't seen Trapper, Earl was in his office last I saw."

"Thanks Fred, talk later." I went down the hallway to Earl's office, and he was sitting back in his chair reading a book. "Trying to improve your mind?" I said.

He jumped from his concentration, "No, it's a book on gambling and card dealing. I have to help with surveillance in the Flamingo casino. They have a suspected cheat, but he knows all the employees, so they wanted an outside investigator to watch him."

I tossed the brochure on his desk. "Feel like going back to Detroit to a big convention for private eyes?"

He picked up the paper and glanced it over as I sat on the side chair of his desk.

"Interesting. This is next month, are you going?"

"I haven't talked to Penny yet, but I'm sure I'll be going whether she does or not."

"Don't be so sure you'll go alone," came a voice from behind me at the door. It was Penny.

**

Chapter 2

I stood quickly as Penny strode into the room. "Hey, beautiful. I guess Lacey spoiled the surprise."

"She mentioned something about a private eye convention back in Detroit. But she said I should talk to you about it," she replied to my stammering. I hated being surprised by her.

"Have a seat, and I'll explain," I said and pulled over another chair to Earl's desk. He was grinning, probably enjoying my discomfort. Penny sat and waited. I sat next to her and showed her the brochure before talking.

She went through the thing, nodding her head and smiling. "Just about every occupation for men has a convention where they can go and party, pick up hookers and drink themselves into a stupor. Is this going to be one?"

"I couldn't say, this convention is the first of its kind. I've never been to one, so I don't know what will go on," I replied hoping she'd let it go.

"Well, I guess I'll have to go along to see that you behave," Penny said, smiling wryly.

I could see Earl stifling a laugh. "Well, that's fine with me. I have no intentions of getting crazy. So you're good to go?"

"I'll have to talk to Gordy about taking the time off from my show, but I'm sure it can be arranged. Will everyone here be able to go?"

"Depends on their cases. If they can get them finished in time, they can go. I can see about another private jet to fly us back to Michigan."

"I hope so, I'll never fly commercial again after that trip we took to the Cayman Islands. That was a disgrace."

"It was. Now, you have to call Gordy and get it set up. I'll talk to the rest of the crew to see who all will be going," I said, relieved she agreed so easily.

"Going where?" Trapper said from the door.

"Hey, Will. Check this out and let me know if you want to go with us." I handed the brochure to Trapper, and he looked it over.

"I already know about this. I have a friend who's on the committee putting this on and he emailed me about it."

"Why didn't you mention it to us?" I asked.

"I just got the email this morning at home before coming in. So I couldn't tell you. Now I am. So who all is going?"

"I am and Penny is willing. Deacon is going to talk to Lynn and Earl hasn't made up his mind yet," I said.

"If I'm not working, I'll go," Earl said.

"All I need now is to let Buck know, and then I'll arrange for a jet," I said, standing up. "I'll go tell Lacey that she can go with us or take a vacation. I noticed they'll have a seminar for office workers to improve their jobs with report filing. Lacey could use that, if she wants to go. She hasn't taken a vacation in years, so it's up to her."

I left the room, but Penny followed me out. "Don't go running off," she said as she caught up to me.

"I'm not running off. This is not a huge building, where would I run off to?" I defended.

"You'd find someplace to hide. So shall we call your family and let them know we'll be coming back?"

"Let's wait until I have everything arranged. I don't want to get anyone excited, and then have our plans fall apart."

We entered the front lobby and over to Lacey's desk. "Lacey, would you like to go with us to this convention?" I asked as she looked up.

Her expression was one of surprise. "I don't know. I have Mac and Jessie to worry about, and Jessie is still in school. I'd hate to pull her out."

"This thing is next month after the kids get out of school. I'm sure Buck would let Mac take the time off to go with us. You and your family could take this as a vacation."

"Wow, a vacation in Detroit," she said sarcastically.

"There's a lot to see and do out there. I can recommend a number of things to do, and I'll even arrange for outings for you guys."

She thought on it. "I'll talk to Mac and see what he says. Thanks."

I turned to Penny. She asked, "Is this going to be as much trouble as when we took everyone back to Michigan for our reunion?"

"We managed to get everyone back there without too much trouble. I have faith that if we follow the same plan that this will work."

"Okay, I'm leaving it to you so don't mess up," she said and kissed me on the cheek.

"I'm so happy that you have faith in me. I'll show you I can do it again," I said.

"Is Lynn in?" Penny asked me.

"No, she's home nursing your namesake. Little Penny has the flu."

"Oh no. I hope she's all right. The flu is going around, and half our stage crew is out with it."

"I hope you stayed away from those who were ill," I said.

"If they were ill, they shouldn't have been in the studio. I'm going home to get my suitcases out to figure what I'll need to take with me."

"Penny dear, it's a month away. You don't need to…Oh, never mind. You'll pack no matter what I say, so go have fun. But only two suitcases to take along. You've been through this before."

"I know and I'll adjust." She kissed me and went out.

I turned to Lacey and said, "I have the feeling this will be another fiasco. I better go into my office and meditate."

"Have a nice nap, boss," she said as I went back through the glass doors toward my office, ignoring her comment. Even though she was right.

I found Willy already on the couch sleeping. "Hey, dog, that's my spot. Move over."

I was getting ready to move the dog when Buck came in. "Hey Jimmy, you aren't getting ready to rest, are you?" he said in his booming voice. Buck was a big man, a full head taller than

I was. I first knew him from when we were working as security guards years ago. Our friendship lasted all these years, and he and I had shared a number of adventures together.

"Trapper said you wanted to see me?" he asked.

I handed him the brochure from my desk and told him about the convention.

"Sure, I'd love to go along if you are getting a jet to take us. I'd like to see my brothers and family again. Will the timing work out?"

"I'll get with Lacey and arrange a cutoff date for new clients. It will take a bit of maneuvering, but I think we can do it."

"Wow, a convention for private investigators. That's exciting. Is this just for Detroit area P.I.s or is it bigger than that?"

"I don't know how far this is going. I'm surprised that they invited us, although Trapper has a friend on the committee. It could be that we got invited because of him. I guess we'll see when we get there."

"This will be a good chance to meet other investigators. You may even make some new friends."

**

Chapter 3

Doyle came through the back door of his building and over to Marge, his receptionist and office wiz. He handed her his reports from a domestic cheating case he finished.

"Can you make something out of this mess? The husband gave me a good run, making sure he could have his little affair without being caught. But he didn't count on me. I got a lot of good photos too. Store those in the file. Where's Oscar?" he asked.

"Oscar is out getting his driver's license renewed," Marge replied.

"Is it his birthday? Doyle asked.

"It was two weeks ago. I didn't know until he told me this morning. He never mentioned it, and I scolded him."

Doyle laughed and said, "We should get a cake for him, devil's food if they have it." Marge agreed as Doyle went to his desk and picked up the mail. He sorted out the bills from the junk, when he saw a brightly colored folded flyer. He read the front and smiled.

"Seems there's a big convention for private investigators coming here in Detroit," he called to Marge.

"When and where?" she asked.

"Next month at the MGM Grand Hotel. This looks interesting," he said as he took the brochure to Marge. "Go ahead and make reservations for Oscar and me. Put yourself down if you want to go, too. I see they have seminars for investigative office staff. You may learn some new tricks."

Marge opened the brochure and said, "It looks like it may be fun. I've never been to a convention, although my late husband, Max, attended a few police conventions. I doubt they got any business done, but he enjoyed going. This convention may be a way of my making up for it."

The back door opened, and Doyle turned, expecting to see Oscar. It was Poppy, Doyle's girlfriend and an investigator for an insurance company.

"Hey, doll, what's up?" he asked her as she came up and planted a big kiss on him. "Well, that was nice. Any special occasion?"

"Nope, just happy to see you," she replied. "Did you get your invite to the investigator's convention?"

"I did just now. You got one too?" Doyle asked.

"They sent one to our office for the investigators. I'm the only one who's going. They figure they can get rid of me for a few days that way."

"I keep telling you to get your private license and come work here. We have enough business to keep you busy."

Private Eye Murders

"I don't know if I can work with you during the day and go home to you at night. Too much Doyle to handle," she said with a laugh.

"We could stop shacking up, that would settle half the problem," Doyle said.

"We don't shack up; that sounds like male ego talking. We share our abode together, loving and living."

"Okay, I'll give you that," Doyle said. "We could agree to avoid each other during the day."

"How long do you think that will last? Besides, if we ever break up, I'd have to quit working for you. Then where would I go? I have a job now, even though I'm not crazy about it."

"Well, let's see how we do living together, and then you can decide."

The back door opened again, and Oscar came in. Doyle whispered to Poppy that it was Oscar's birthday. She grinned and went to Oscar, grabbing on to him and gave him a lip lock that even Doyle could feel. She backed off and said, "Happy birthday, Oscar."

He turned beet red and grinned. "Don't forget me next year," he said and went to his desk. "Well, I renewed my driver's license for another year. Although I had a problem with the eye test, they almost flunked me. Now I have to go get my eyes checked."

"You're getting old Oscar," Doyle said. "Take care of it, and then you'll be fine."

"Sure, you don't have to wear glasses," Oscar said.

Changing the subject, Doyle said, "On another note, I got a brochure today for a big convention for private eyes, that's going to be held here in Detroit next month. I told Marge to sign us up."

"I heard about that from a friend of mine at the 5-2 precinct. I ran into him yesterday, and he mentioned it. He can't go, it's only for private investigators. He asked me if I was going, I told him I hadn't heard about it."

"Marge has the information if you're interested. I think it would be good. They have seminars on surveillance and filling out reports properly. You could use that."

"That's what we have Marge for, to get our reports in order," Oscar said.

Doyle didn't reply since he gave Marge his report earlier to fill out. "It's going to be at the MGM Grand; that should be a big deal. Just for the fun of it, I may get a room in the hotel."

"You just want a room closer to the bar, so you don't have far to go," Oscar said with a big grin.

Poppy said, "I'll be there to take him to his room. He'll be in good hands."

"No comment," Doyle said.

The front door opened, and a woman came in. Marge asked if she needed help.

"I'd like to hire a private investigator to follow my husband. Are your investigators discreet?" she asked.

Doyle came over to her and said, "Ma'am, we are very discreet. Please follow me." He took her to his desk as Poppy went to Marge.

"Are you going to the convention?" Poppy asked Marge.

"Oh, hell, yes. I need to cut loose and have a good time. I know these conventions are for business, but they do a lot of partying also. I haven't cut loose in…well, a lot of years." She started laughing quietly, so as not to disturb Doyle and his new client.

"Marge, I'll be there and we can go party together. Doyle has Oscar to run with, so we can cut loose as you say."

Oscar came up to the women and said to Poppy, "Do you think I'd look dorky in glasses?"

"Oscar, you would look very distinctive in glasses. You'll attract a better type of woman with the right glasses. Get the kind that make you look dangerous."

Oscar smiled and asked Marge, "Put me down for the convention. I'll go tomorrow and see about glasses."

Doyle finished with the woman, and they came over to Marge's desk as Poppy and Oscar moved away.

"Marge, will you take Mrs. Randall's retainer?" Marge agreed as Doyle turned back to the woman. "I'll start on this tomorrow morning. Don't worry, I'll nail him if he's cheating."

She thanked Doyle and paid Marge the fee. Doyle went to Oscar and Poppy, "Now we have to think about the convention and what kind of party hats we'll need."

"I hardly think it will be that much fun," Poppy said. "I'm sure you'll learn some new things and meet interesting people who share your occupation. I want to go to the lectures on insurance fraud, which is my field. They have good people speaking on how to go on surveillance and stakeouts. You can use that."

"Sure," Oscar said. "You may even make new friends."

**

Chapter 4

Gus hadn't gotten around to leaving his house yet. He was falling behind today. He wasn't worried, he had only a few clients and since he worked alone, he couldn't handle too many investigating cases.

His daughter, Angela, had already gone to work at the hospital where she was a nurse. The house was quiet, except for Fritz wolfing down his dog food in the kitchen. Gus had finally tracked down Fritz's background in the military. The big German Shepherd had started in a K-9 unit in Washington, D.C., and he became a highly trained combat dog. He was meant to sniff out explosives, drugs, and track the bad guys. He knew when to attack a man holding a gun if the man was the enemy. Fritz had been given a couple awards for his service that Gus would have to track down. They'd make a nice plaque on the wall. Not that Fritz cared.

Gus looked at the clock on the wall and saw that he should have opened his office thirty minutes ago. He wasn't concerned, he knew people would come back. There weren't a lot of private investigators in Detroit that worked as cheaply as he did, so people seemed to like hiring him.

He figured his friend, Bernie would be calling soon. He knew Bernie from when they worked together in the military police in Germany. Two years of putting up with Gus had worn down Bernie into becoming a friend. Bernie was a full-blooded Native-American Sioux and still held on to his heritage. He needed the inherited patience to work with Gus. Bernie was a homicide Lieutenant for the Detroit Police and was a lot of help for Gus on his cases.

Gus went to get a bowl of cereal, something he rarely ate, but he was hungry this morning. He turned and almost dropped the bowl of flakes, no milk, when he saw the man standing in the doorway to his kitchen.

"Damn it, Bernie. You stopped picking my office lock, now you're going to pick my house lock," he yelled at the man.

"I was concerned about your health. You hadn't shown up at your office, so I came here to see if you had died in your sleep," Bernie said with a grin. "I am relieved."

"Well, you almost gave me a heart attack. You're lucky I didn't have my gun on me," Gus said as he sat to eat his cereal.

"Why? You can't shoot straight anyway." Bernie said as he sat at the table. "You don't have any cases to work today?"

"Not at the moment. I have a little money stashed away from the rock star case. So I'm not rushing into anything," Gus said.

"I'm surprised rock star Tracy paid you. She wasn't the nicest person to deal with."

"Actually, her recording company paid me. I reminded them that her life was saved to make them more money. They were happy to pay me off," Gus said, munching on dry cereal flakes.

"You could put milk on that," Bernie said.

"I'm out of milk. What are you doing out so early?"

Bernie tossed a folded paper to Gus. "Here, you may be interested in this. It's a private investigator convention in Detroit next month.

You may learn how to be a better P.I. and make some money."

Gus picked up the brochure and studied it as Bernie picked at Gus' dry cereal. Gus pushed the bowl to Bernie and said, "Here, enjoy."

Gus spread out the brochure on the table and was looking at all the features of the convention. "How did you get this?" Gus asked.

"It was in your mailbox out front," Bernie said.

Gus turned it to see his name and address was on it. "Interesting. They didn't send it to my office, they sent it here. How did they know where to send it?"

"They're private investigators, Gus. They find people. Besides, I gave them your address," Bernie said with a wry grin.

"You know someone running this thing?"

"Sure, a friend who's a retired cop and now a P.I. in Detroit. He's one of four who are putting this on. I think you should go."

Gus was turning the brochure over and coughed, "Have you seen how much they want to attend this dog and pony show. Six hundred for the four days."

"That's cheap, besides you can afford it. You should still have money stashed away from the missing princess case. Or did you blow it all?"

"I still have it. I put it away for my retirement. I guess I can take some out to pay for this. Can you attend?"

"Nope, not officially. I'm a cop, and this is for private investigators. Although I was asked to be there to talk about the relationship between cops and P.I.s. Giving my expert advice on how investigators should ask the police nicely for information on a suspect. I have lots of experience in dealing with you, bugging me for info."

"I don't bug, do I?"

"No comment," Bernie said and sat back.

"Thanks," Gus said. "This is being held at the MGM Grand, fancy digs for a convention. They couldn't rent a V.F.W. hall to hold it?"

"May as well go all out for the first of its kind. While the private eyes go to seminars, their wives can go gambling."

"Sure, it's a win-win for the MGM Grand. Is this thing open to just Detroit area P.I.s or is it a big deal?"

"My friend told me they've sent out brochures all over the country to the major cities. It should be a big deal."

"Fine, I'll go. Now I have to get ready for work." Gus stood and put the bowl in the sink. "I'll be out shortly."

"Gus," Bernie said as Gus was leaving the room.

"What?" he replied stopping at the doorway.

"Nice duckie print pajama bottoms," Bernie said trying not to laugh.

"They were a gift from Angela, so suck it up." Bernie went out of the room as Bernie was laughing.

An hour later, Gus, Bernie and Fritz were in Gus' office. Gus checked the answering machine and wrote down the call information. Nothing earth shattering, just questions on what Gus could do as a private investigator. He'd respond back later to a couple of the serious sounding calls.

Fritz was on his dog bed watching Bernie and Gus at the desk. Gus was looking through his mail that he picked up from the mail slot on the front door. He sorted through the mail and said, "They sent me a brochure here too. They must have money for postage."

"Bulk rates, Gus. They save on postage. Are you going to turn in your reservations for the convention?"

"I guess I'll take care of that today, so I don't put it off. Can I sign up for it online?"

"Does it say you can in the brochure?"

Gus flipped through the folder and said, "Yep, it's right here. They have a website, too." Gus turned on his computer and waited for it to boot up. "Did you ever think we'd be taking care of business by computers?"

"Gus, my ancestors did business by smoke signals. They never dreamed of working through the internet. You should have a good time at this convention, you may even make new friends."

**

Chapter 5

One month later, Jim had commitments from those who were going to the convention. The firm stopped taking cases about two weeks before and everyone was taking the time off to prepare for the trip and to goof around. Penny had her two suitcases packed and sitting by the front door.

"I have everything I'll need while out there. I may take advantage of the spa and get a makeover" Penny said as she stood staring at her luggage.

"Makeover? Can they make you look like Sophia Vergara?" I asked, staying far enough away to avoid being hit.

"That's wishful thinking, buster. Now stop it. I'll still be the beautiful woman you married. Now you could use a makeover. I'd be happy with George Clooney."

"He's married now, dear," I responded.

"So are you. Who's finally agreed to go on this journey?"

"Well, Buck, Earl without Paula, Trapper without Samantha, Deacon without Lynn, and Lacey with Mac and Jessie. Then you and me. I asked Fred, but he said he'd pass."

"All those men going without their women? They're going to turn this into a wild party. Lynn isn't going?" Penny asked.

"She's said the baby is too young to travel and party at a convention. She also told me, when Deacon wasn't nearby, that she could use the time alone without him hanging around and fussing over her and the baby. Don't tell Deacon that."

"She can get together with Paula and Sam and have her own party. Maybe I'll stay and join them." Penny said with a grin.

"What, and miss out staying at the Detroit MGM Grand Hotel and using all their amenities, like the spa?"

"I can do that here. We're in Sin City, sweetie, where you can get any luxury you'd want. But I would like to see your family again. So Lacey and I are the only women going, fine," she said then went into the kitchen followed by Willy.

I went into the bedroom to get my bag packed with the clothes I picked out earlier. I had the commercial jet all arranged and the reservations for everyone at the hotel and the convention. I put it all on the company account since this was a business trip. I could write it off on my taxes that way.

Penny entered the bedroom holding a spoon and held it up to my mouth.

"Taste," she said as I eyed the liquid in the spoon.

"What is it?" I said warily, knowing Penny's culinary skills were disastrous at times.

"Just open your mouth and take your medicine," she ordered.

"Are you going to poison me finally, to get my money?" I said as I put my mouth on the spoon and took it in. "Hey, that's good. What is it?"

"It's a soup that a chef made on my show today. I brought some home," she replied.

"Tell him to teach you to make that."

"He did, I'll make some when we get back from our trip." She turned and left the bedroom. Willy was sitting at my feet, looking dejected.

I picked him up and said, "Sorry, buddy, we've neglected you. But you're going back on a jet. You had a good time with the flight attendants last time we flew. You old hound dog, you." I put him down and continued packing.

Private Eye Murders

The front door bell rang, and I went out to see who it was. Penny was already at the door, and she let Buck come in.

"Hey Jim, are you ready to go back home?" he asked with his usual smile.

"This is our home, Buck. Back there is where we used to live. Our family is there, but you and everyone we know here is also our family." I said.

"Well said, my friend. I've got my bags in the company van, shall I put yours in with them?" he asked.

Penny said, "You can put mine in, Jim is still packing."

"I'll be done soon enough. Besides, we have to wait for Trapper and Earl. Lacey said they'd meet us at the airport."

Penny pointed out her bags and Buck hefted them to take out. "What did you pack? Bricks?"

"Just clothes and a few items to make myself look beautiful," she replied.

"She's taking all her cosmetics from her dressing table. Don't strain yourself, Buck."

She swung her arm to whack me, but I moved away. "I did not pack everything, just the essentials."

Buck laughed and went out to the van with the bags. I went to the door and saw Trapper drive up in his jeep. He had Earl and Deacon with him. I went out to greet them followed by Penny and Willy.

Trapper parked on the side of the drive so Buck could get the van out. I had called for a limo to take us to the airport, so we didn't need to leave our cars at the terminal. The van would take the luggage.

"Buck, help me with the bags," Trapper said to Buck as he put Penny's bags in the van. The two of them took the luggage from Trapper's Jeep and put them in the van.

"So, are you excited to be going back?" Earl asked me.

"I'm looking forward to it," I said. "Seeing the family is going to be the highlight. The convention will be fun and a learning experience."

"Oh sure, you and the bad boys will be in jail by the next day after we get there. I'm not bailing you out." Penny smiled and went back in the house. I looked over and saw that Willy was fertilizing the lawn. That was good, so he wouldn't have to go on the five hour flight to Detroit.

Deacon came over and asked, "Do you have a limo picking us up in Detroit?"

"Yep, it will take us to the MGM Grand Hotel. I have the rooms reserved for the three nights we'll be there." I said.

Trapper said from the van, "Last time we went back, we ended up staying longer to find the killer of your friends at the reunion."

"I doubt we'll have any problems. There'll be tons of private investigators that can solve any crimes. We'll be enjoying ourselves and learning. No investigating."

"Famous last words," Buck muttered. "Go get your bags packed Jim, we have to be at McCarron commercial hangers in an hour."

"Yes, mother," I said laughing and went into the house leaving Buck, Trapper and Earl alone. I entered the bedroom and saw Penny packing a carry-on bag. "You just don't quit, do you?"

"What? These are those last minute things I forgot. I'm allowed a carry-on bag, aren't I?" she said.

"Yes, dear, you are. I hope we don't overload the jet," I said.

"It will be all right. Did you call your mother?"

"I did this morning. She's all excited and said she'd call my brother and my son. I told her I didn't know what day we would visit, so not to make plans until we get there."

"We have sight-seeing to do, too."

"Penny, I grew up there, I've seen it all. You may find things to see, but I'll be busy with the convention. I doubt we'll see much of each other. You'll be in the spa and I'll be learning to save money for the business and track criminals."

"You'll be busy socializing with the other P.I.s, so I hope you meet a lot of nice people.

**

Chapter 6

Doyle, Oscar, Poppy and Marge approached the main reception desk of the MGM Grand Hotel and Doyle gave their names to the girl behind the counter. They had to sign in and show their IDs.

"Yes, Mr. Doyle, we have all of your party together on the eighth floor overlooking the downtown area. Give me a second, and I'll have your door cards ready." She went about preparing the key cards as they were looking around the lobby.

"I've never been in here. Lots of marble all around. It looks expensive," Oscar said.

"It's on the firm, so it's a tax write off," Doyle said. "Just enjoy your stay and don't worry about it."

"Arthur, is there a restaurant in this building?" Marge asked.

The girl behind the counter heard her and said, "We have a number of restaurants for you to enjoy and a night club."

"Oh, a night club. I know what I'll be doing later," Marge laughed.

"I'll be your bodyguard, Marge," Poppy said.

"Who'll guard your body?" Doyle asked Poppy.

"I'm hoping you will," she said with a sly grin.

The counter girl said, "Here are your key cards, enjoy your stay. I'll have your bags brought up to you." She signaled to a man in uniform, and he went to the cart carrying their bags. He went off with the cart leaving the group standing at the counter.

"Where's he going?" Oscar said.

"He's taking the bags up in the service elevator, he'll meet you at your rooms. You can find the passenger elevators around the corner," the girl said pointing the direction.

Doyle and his party went around to the elevators and waited for it to arrive. The doors finally opened, and everyone got in the car. Just as the doors were closing, Doyle heard someone yell to hold the elevator. He reached out and stopped the doors. They opened back up, and two men, and a German Shepherd on a leash rushed up and got in.

"Thanks," said a man with grayish hair who looked to be in his fifties. The other man with him, Doyle noted, looked to be Native-American. He had jet black hair tied in a short ponytail, taller than everyone in the elevator and was probably the same age as his smaller friend. The big man leaned back against the wall of the elevator, crossed his arm over his chest and smiled at Doyle. Doyle glanced down at the man's belt where he saw a gold shield clipped to it. He was a cop, Doyle realized. Probably a detective judging from the gold badge.

"Hi, are you from a precinct in Detroit?" Doyle asked the big man.

The man held his hand out and said, "Bernie Longmire, Homicide, and you are Art Doyle. I remember you from when you shot the mayor."

"I just grazed him and I'd like to forget that. What precinct are you from? I was with the 4-6 before I quit."

"I'm in the 3-8, and this man is Gus Mackie, private investigator, the dog is Fritz," he said, pointing to Gus. Fritz, sitting at Gus' feet, was wearing a vest that read in big letter on the sides, K-9.

Doyle held out his hand to Gus, and they shook. Gus said, "I'm not as famous as you, but I survive in this crazy world of P.I. and I do alright."

"We all survive in this world, Gus. These people are my friends and co-workers. This is Oscar Drew, my associate. Behind him is Marge

Wayne, my office manager, and this beautiful woman is Poppy Drake, an insurance investigator. Are you staying in the hotel, Gus?"

"I decided that I need to pamper myself and stay in the hotel. I got a luxury suite after Bernie threatened me to spend a little money," he laughed and looked at Bernie. Bernie grinned but remained silent. "I have a house nearby, but this is more exciting staying here."

"We all live in Detroit, but it's good to enjoy the high life. This convention should be interesting. We're signed up for the full tour. All four days and three nights of learning what we're doing wrong," Doyle said with a grin.

Bernie spoke, "Gus usually does things his way and occasionally succeeds without my help."

"Are you part of this wing-ding, Bernie?" Oscar asked.

"I'm speaking on how you investigators can get the police to cooperate with your cases," Bernie said.

"It does help when you have a cop on your side," Doyle said.

"Or were a former cop," Gus added.

"We're not all that lucky, but that helps. What floor are you on?" Doyle asked.

"Nine, overlooking the slums," Gus joked. "But, I won't be looking out the windows, I don't like heights."

"We're on eight, just below you. Maybe we can get together for a drink in the bar later?" Doyle asked.

Gus grinned and said, "Sounds good to me. I don't want to start the convention tomorrow morning without a couple beers in me. Bernie keeps an eye on me so I don't over-drink. I had problems with it years ago."

"Well, we'll keep an eye on you too." Doyle handed Gus his card. "My cell phone number is on there if you and Bernie decide to join us."

"Thanks," Gus said as the doors to the elevator opened. "Here's your floor," Gus said to Doyle.

Private Eye Murders

Everyone said their goodbyes and departed the elevator leaving Gus, Bernie and Fritz alone. The doors closed and Gus said, "Nice people." Bernie just grunted and smiled.

In the hallway, Doyle handed out the key cards to Oscar and Marge. Their bags arrived with the bellhop, and he parked it in the middle of the hallway. He stood there waiting until Doyle realized why. He took out a ten and handed it to the man. The man smiled, thanked him and left.

"Okay, grab your bags and get unpacked. We'll meet out here in an hour and go get some food," Doyle said as Poppy removed her bags from the cart. Doyle took his bags and used the key card in their room door. The door unlocked, and they went in. Doyle looked back at Oscar and Marge opening their room doors and taking their bags in. Doyle closed the door and turned.

Poppy grabbed on to him and said, "We have an hour to defile this room, so get undressed." He laughed as Poppy stripped down to her underwear and headed to the huge bed. Doyle didn't hesitate and followed her.

Gus, Fritz, and Bernie got off one floor up and went to Gus' room. "You can stay here tonight if you'd like," Gus told Bernie.

Bernie was looking around the opulent room and said, "Don't tempt me. I have to change for work in the morning."

"Are you going to join Doyle and his friends in a drink tonight?" Gus asked.

"I may, but I'll have to take Fritz home with me. He can't stay here overnight."

"Why not?" Gus asked.

"Gus, do you want to go down nine floors to let Fritz take a dump out front?"

Gus thought on that. "I should have left him with Angela. Can you take him there?"

"I do think Fritz would prefer that over crapping on the street," Bernie said with a laugh.

**

Chapter 7

Our flight back to Detroit was going smoothly. Everyone was comfortable and Willy was enjoying the flight attendants playing with him. Penny was relaxed while reading a magazine about gambling. I didn't know why, we lived in the gambling capital of the United States and she never gambled there. Maybe she felt it was a new adventure.

Lacey was sitting with Jessie, in the window seat, as the young girl was watching the scenery go by below. Mac was with Buck, Earl and Trapper in the back seats talking about what they plan to do in Detroit. I hope Trapper wasn't going to pull any pranks at the convention.

We were about ten minutes out of Metro Airport just below Detroit and I hoped the limo service was there, including a van for our luggage. Finally, we were instructed to buckle up for the landing and put our seats up. I was watching out the window at the ground below coming up fast. The jet touched down safely without much of a bump and taxied into the area for commercial business jets.

We were all stretching after the almost five-hour flight and headed to the door to go down the ramp. We left Vegas at 9 am but the flight brought us to Michigan by 5 pm. There was a three-hour difference between Michigan and Nevada so it was now 2 pm back in Vegas and Detroit was three hours later, so it was 5 pm. The difference always threw me off. It was worse than daylight savings time.

"That was a nice flight," Penny said.

"You read most of the way," I said to her. "You hardly looked out the window at the passing states. That's the best part of flying."

"I'll watch it on the way back," she replied as we went into the terminal to collect our bags. They hadn't off-loaded the bags yet, so we had to wait.

A half hour later, we were all loaded into the limo and bags safely stored in the van. I told the driver where we needed to go.

"Yes, sir," he replied. "I've driven many a person to the MGM Grand. Going for vacation or business?"

"Convention, for private investigators," I explained.

"Well, that sounds like fun," he came back.

He pulled out as the van followed, and drove over to Interstate 94, then out to the John Lodge Freeway, south to the hotel. He pulled up to the main entrance and we got out. The bags were being put on a couple carts by Buck and Earl. Mac and Lacey helped with the bags. Trapper and Deacon came with me and Penny into the lobby and up to the reservation counter.

"Good afternoon, folks. Do you have reservations?" the girl at the counter asked.

I took out the sheet of paper that I had written everything down for the hotel arrangements and showed her. "I reserved three rooms, my wife and myself in one, four men in another and a family of three in the last." I had Buck, Earl, Deacon and Trapper together in one room. They would have to put up with it. Lacey, Mac, and Jessie had a room and Penny and I had another. It was the cheapest way I could set it up, short of putting everybody in one room.

She smiled and typed on her keyboard, looking at the monitor. "I have all of you in adjoining rooms on the fifth floor, Southside. I'll get your key cards ready.

I looked back as Buck and Earl pushed the luggage carts in, followed by Lacey and Jessie. I didn't see Mac.

"Lacey, where's Mac?" I asked as she came up.

"He left his gym bag in the limo, so he went to get it. He'll be in shortly," she replied as Mac entered the lobby with the bag.

The girl finished up and handed me the key cards. I asked her, "Can you tell me where the private investigators convention will be?"

"It's going to be held in the Grand Ballroom. I'll give you a map of the hotel so you can find it easily." She reached to a rack, took out a brochure and spread it out on the counter. "You are here, and the Grand Ballroom is here, just follow the route and you can't miss it. I'm sure there will be many people going in that direction, so follow them."

"Thanks," I said. The woman signaled to a man and he went to take the luggage carts. Buck wasn't letting the man take the carts.

"Sir, I'm just taking them to your floor, I'm not stealing them. If you'd like, you can go with me."

Buck agreed and the two men wheeled the carts to the service elevator. I told everyone to follow and we went to the elevators the girl had pointed out. We arrived on the fifth floor and found our rooms. I gave the key cards to Trapper and Mac and they went to the assigned rooms. Penny was standing at our door waiting for me to open it.

I called to Trapper and Mac about going to dinner in an hour. They agreed. Buck and the bellhop came down the hall to us with the carts and we took our luggage off them. I tipped the man and he left.

"Where's my tip?" Buck asked.

"I'll give you a tip, don't gamble," I said and went to my room. I put the card in the slot and the lock gave way. I opened the door and Penny and I went in.

"Nice room," Penny said, as she walked around.

"It better be nice for what this room cost."

"Don't be a Scrooge, this is an adventure. I intend to have a great time. You'll be busy with your childish convention while I'll be luxuriating in the spa."

"All four days?" I asked.

"If I can. At night, I'll be dancing away in the night club."

"Without me?"

"No, you can come along to pay for my drinks." She grinned and went to the bed. "Care to join me?"

An hour later, we dressed and went out to the lobby. I knocked on the door of the four men and Earl answered.

"Are you room service?" he asked me.

"No, you have to get your own room service. Are you ready to go get dinner?"

"Yep, the crackers on the jet didn't fill me up." He turned back to Trapper and Buck and told them it was time to eat.

"Are Penny and Jim finished fooling around in their room?" Trapper yelled.

"Mind your own business, Will. You could have brought Sam, but you wanted to be free to party."

"Bingo," he yelled back. "I intend to have fun and not drag a woman around the whole weekend."

"Fine, if you guys want to eat, go find the restaurant yourself. I'm getting Lacey, Jessie and Mac and going to eat." I turned away and left them. I went to Mac's door and knocked. Jessie answered. Jessie was growing up so fast since Penny and I first took her in after her abusive father was murdered by the Vegas Vigilante. Lacey and Mac took her in as foster parents after they got married.

"Hi, Grandpa Jim. We're ready to go eat." She turned to yell back into the room that I was there. Everyone was yelling it seemed. This was going to be a noisy weekend.

**

Chapter 8

I gathered everyone and we headed down to one of the restaurants. I had called ahead and reserved a table for us so we could get in and out without a hassle.

We came off the elevator to the main floor, and I saw a tall, dark-skinned man, not black, but well-tanned. He had a ponytail and a German Shepherd on a leash, walking through the lobby to the main entrance. He went out and I wondered if he was a cop, the dog had a K-9 vest on. I'm sure he was a Native-American and wondered if he was here for the convention.

We entered the restaurant and I gave my name. They took us to a table and we sat, then ordered.

Private Eye Murders

This hotel and casino didn't seem to have the excitement that any Vegas hotel and casino had. Vegas had thousands of people going in and out of town every day, so the excitement was there. Thousands of people wandering the Strip going from casino to casino. Many with drinks in their hands, as it wasn't illegal. The MGM Grand here catered to people from around Detroit and Canada across the Detroit River, and a few people coming in from all over the world. Atlantic City and Vegas were the big hot spots for gambling and other diversions. All over the country smaller casinos were available due to Native-Americans taking advantage of the law.

"What's on your devious little mind?" Penny whispered in my ear as we were waiting for our food.

"I was just thinking about the difference between here and Vegas," I replied.

"Not quite as exciting, is it?" she asked.

"My thoughts exactly. In Vegas, it's a way of life and the city has that vitality that makes it Sin City. Here, it's just Detroit with a big casino. People don't wander the streets, too far to go between casinos. This is the Motor City, not Sin City," I explained my feelings.

"It used to be Murder City," Trapper added. "Although I think it's dropped in the rankings."

"Detroit has a bad rep. The city isn't all that bad," Earl piped up, joining the conversation. "When I was a homicide cop here, the crime rate was high, but the downtown streets were still safe to walk."

"If you were in a group of people," Trapper said. "You don't walk alone around the city, you're asking for trouble."

"Okay, I'll give you that. But it's dangerous in most big cities. Some safer than others, but still dangerous," Earl said.

"I liked being a cop here in the suburbs," Deacon finally spoke. "It was safer, and fewer murders."

"Mostly traffic citations and domestic abuse calls," Trapper said. "You and I were in the same precinct. Which was fine with me. I never could have worked out of Detroit."

"It's all still work, no matter what the crime," I said. "Trapper, you had a number of major crimes when I was there."

"Sure, you caused most of the crimes as I remember," Deacon laughed.

"I did not," I defended. "I may have been involved in solving a number of crimes, only because the police couldn't handle it."

"Don't go there, Jim. I can give you a rundown on all your blunders," Trapper said with a smirk.

Our food came in time to cut our discussion off. We sat eating and not talking much. When we finished, I paid with the company charge card and we left.

We wandered the hotel and found the Grand Ballroom, where the convention was to be held. They had it all decorated and ready for the private eyes to converge in the morning. We went into the casino and it was busy for the time of day. But my internal clock was off from the time difference between Vegas and Detroit. It was now after six in the evening and only three back in Vegas.

Lacey and Mac couldn't bring Jessie in the casino, she was underage. They said they were going to their room to relax.

"Care to take a chance at the Black Jack table?" Earl asked me. I declined.

"I've never been much for gambling, even in Vegas," I replied.

"He's a wuss," Penny said, poking me in the ribs.

"Yes, my dear, I am when it comes to losing large sums of money. I can use it better on toys. I think I've had enough of the tour, let's go rescue Willy from the bathroom. I'm sure he's not a happy dog."

"Well, I'm going to see how much I can win or lose," Earl said.

"I'll join you," Trapper added. "Come on, Buck. You can protect our winnings." The three men went off leaving Deacon, who also declined.

"I don't have the money like single guys do. Paying bills and raising the baby taps me out," Deacon said morosely.

"Deacon, if you don't make a big deal out of it to the others, I'll give you a raise. Although I'll have to give Lacey one or she'll have a fit that I'm giving you one."

"Well, thank you Jim, I can use it. But I still won't gamble. I'm going back to my room and get some rest for tomorrow," Deacon said.

"Bright and early, I'll come by to get you," I said and he went off. I turned to Penny. "Now, shall we go see what our baby is doing? Did you bring some food to give him?"

"I wrapped up the fish I didn't eat. It was too much for me. They sure piled it on."

"Yep, I'll give the restaurant five stars. Great meal and lots of it. I always hated those restaurants that put tiny portions on your plate and drown it in parsley. Shall we go?"

I took Penny back to the elevators and waited for the car to come. The tall man came up, without the dog this time.

"Did you lose your dog?" I asked with a smile.

He grinned and said, "I took him home, too much work to have a dog in the hotel."

"We have a dog in our room, but he's a toy Yorkie. Much easier to handle," I said.

"And their messes are smaller, too," he replied.

"Much. I'm Jim Richards and this is my wife, Penny Wickens."

"I know Ms. Wickens from when she had her talk show here in Detroit. I occasionally watch the national show now. I know you too, Jim, I follow the crime news. I'm Bernie Longmire, Detroit Homicide," he said holding out his hand to shake.

"Are you part of the convention?" I asked.

"I'm here to speak about relations between cops and P.I.s. You have an agency in Las Vegas?"

"I do, with a staff of four ex-cops and numerous helpers. It keeps me busy."

"Busy, ha!" Penny burst out laughing. "Bernie, he sits around and takes naps while everyone else works. He's the figurehead of the firm and does the public relations on the news when they break a big case."

"I do more than that. I've been involved in a number of cases that needed my expertise. I saved Vegas twice from a dirty bomb and a deadly virus. What about the deadly sunblock case? I do too work."

Penny looked at Bernie and said, "Yes, he is useful and an inspiration for the others."

"That's better," I said and kissed her cheek.

**

Chapter 9

We pushed the buttons for our floors and the doors closed. "Did you know an Earl Daws?" I asked the man.

"Earl, sure, I remember him. I wasn't in his precinct, but I've heard of him."

"He's working with us. Along with two cops from Clinton Township, and a friend of mine who got his license, along with running our security guard service." I said.

"Sound like you got it all covered. How well do you get along with the local police?"

"One of my associates used to work with Vegas police, before moving to Michigan years ago, and has many friends, who still tolerate him. Another associate married an LVPD homicide Detective and worked his way up to sergeant. They both left Vegas PD to work with me. It's a good team now and we keep busy. I've worked closely with Vegas PD, so we have a good relationship."

"It helps to keep a good relationship so you're not stepping on toes. Many police officers don't like P.I.s hanging around their cases. Cops can be very territorial, and don't like interference from the outside. I have one P.I. who I've known for years and I often help him with his cases. He's not the best investigator, but he manages to hold his own."

"Sure, I'd like to meet him," I said.

"There are going to be a number of investigators you'll meet. It's like a big boy's club."

The doors to the fifth floor opened and I said, "Our floor. Hope to see you again."

"I'm sure you will," he said with a smile.

The doors closed and I said, "Nice guy. Would be helpful to get to know him better."

"Sure, you can have him do your work, too," Penny said with a grin.

"Will you stop that? I do too work." I opened the door and went to let Willy out of the bathroom. It was a safer place to put him so he didn't tear up the suite. He was sleeping on the floor and looked up to me. He jumped up and shot out of the room. I went to clean up his little gift and flushed it in the toilet. I could hear Penny talking to him in the other room.

I came out and they were both sitting on the couch watching the big screen TV. Penny found an old movie with Bogart and Bacall, 'To Have and Have Not' which I'd seen before. I plopped down next to Willy and he moved over to me.

"Good dog, you know who your favorite is," I said as Penny told me to quiet down. She was watching the movie.

After a while we retired to the bedroom letting Willy sleep with us. Penny stripped the bed and replaced the sheets with ones we brought with us. It was a custom we had, to avoid sleeping on sheets that have had thousands of people doing who knows what on them. I put my head back on the pillow and stared at the ceiling.

"Tomorrow, I'm going to find the spa while you go play with your little friends," Penny said quietly.

"They're not little and I hardly know most of them. Maybe I'll make some new friends that can be helpful. We could form a network of investigators to exchange information about our cases. Sort of like the police and FBI have their NCIC."

"Sounds interesting, sweetie. Now go to sleep. I need my beauty rest," she said and rolled over on her side away from me.

Willy snuggled up to me and I said to him quietly, "Looks like the honeymoon is over."

I was woken early by a pounding on the door and stumbled out to see who it was. I looked through the peep hole and it was black. Someone had their hand over it.

"Who is it?" I yelled through the door.

"Room service," came a voice sounding like Earl.

"I didn't order any room service. Go away, Earl."

"Time to get up and go register. I want to get an early start," he said.

I looked at my watch, it was just after eight. I opened the door and said, "I don't think they even start taking registrations until ten. Go away." I closed the door and heard him laughing. I was up now, so I figured I may as well get ready for the day.

Penny was still in bed. I let her sleep, so she could get her beauty rest, although she was beautiful enough. For a sixty-three year old woman she kept her good looks and never resorted to cosmetic surgery. She didn't need it.

I showered and shaved and got dressed as Willy was following me around. Penny was now sitting up in bed watching me dress.

"Does this give you a thrill? Watching me reverse striptease?"

"Not in the least," she said with a smile. "I just like watching you. I'm amazed that I still love you after all we've been through."

"What? The crimes and you being kidnapped numerous times?" I asked.

"That and we have our separate lives that we let each other go about without being petty or jealous. I'm a successful television talk show host and you are a famous private eye. We make a good team."

I thought on that for a moment and agreed. "We are friends and lovers. A good combination for a good marriage. Now I'm going to go find the place to register for the convention. You can go find the spa. If you need anything, call me."

I left her in the bedroom and went to the door. I opened it to find Deacon standing in the hallway. "Are you lost?" I asked.

"No, I'm waiting for Trapper and Buck to get a move on," Deacon said. "Earl left early to go register, but I don't think they started already."

"I was informed it started at ten. Earl can just stand around waiting. Shall we go get some breakfast?" I asked just as Buck came out. "Where's Trapper?"

"He's coming, slowly. I think he drank too much at the bar last night. We met some investigators from Detroit. A guy named Doyle and his partner Oscar. Then we were joined by a man named Gus Mackie and his police friend, Bernie Longmire."

"I already met Longmire, he seems like a decent guy. What time did you get in?"

"Around three. Everyone wanted to get some rest before this thing starts. What's Penny going to do?"

"She's seeking out a spa to relax in," I said as Trapper came out. "Ready to face the world?" I asked him.

"Guide me to the ballroom, I think I had a brain fart," he said.

"Too much drinking. I didn't even have a beer last night," I said.

"That's your tough luck. I had enough for the both of us. I almost slept in but Earl was bouncing around the room getting ready. I almost shot him."

"I'm glad you didn't, we don't need the trouble. I want this weekend to be fun and peaceful. Let's go enjoy ourselves," I said and led the way to the elevators.

We arrived at the Grand Ballroom and there were a number of people already there. Buck tapped me on the shoulder. "That's Art Doyle," he said pointing to a man talking with two women. "Come on, I'll introduce you."

**

Chapter 10

I followed Buck over to the man and women. "Yo, Doyle," Buck called to the man. He turned and smiled.

"Buck, good to see you again," the man said.

"Doyle, this is Jim Richards, owner of Richards Investigations in Las Vegas and my good buddy."

"I remember you, Jim, back when you were chasing the classmate murderers. Word travels fast when there's a manhunt. I used to be in homicide in Detroit and we were on the alert for your perps. Good work catching them."

I shook hands with the man and looked at the women he was talking to.

"This is Marge Wayne, my office manager and all around dangerous woman," he said with a grin. "This is Poppy Drake, insurance investigator, and the love of my life."

"For now," Poppy added.

"Hey, I say it, better believe it," Doyle exclaimed.

"Good to meet all of you. My office manager is wandering around with her husband and daughter. My wife decided to go to a spa, rather than be bored to death by more of my antics in crime detection."

"Your wife is Penny Wickens," Poppy said. "I've seen her show. Are you going to drag her here so we can meet her?"

"She has a mind of her own, but I'll try to drag her," I said as I heard a voice behind me.

"I don't need to be dragged," Penny said, standing behind me. I jumped.

"How does she do that? I hate it when she creeps up behind me," I said and turned to Penny. "I thought you were going to a spa?"

"I was, but they were full, so I came here to bug you," she replied.

I introduced everyone to Penny, and Poppy asked, "Are you going for a spa treatment?"

"I will around two when they have an opening," she said.

"Can you get me in?" Poppy asked.

Marge piped up, "I'd like to get in on that, too."

Penny laughed and said, "I'll call and see what I can do."

There was an announcement that the registration tables were open. We all went to sign in and get our name badges. I saw Earl grinning at me from in the ballroom. He probably bribed someone to let him register early.

Penny and Marge waited back while the men and Poppy went to register.

"Is Poppy an investigator?" Penny asked Marge.

"She works for an insurance company as an investigator, seeking out fraudulent claims. She and Arthur met when she came to appraise the damage to Arthur's cabin, which was blown up by a serial killer."

"Oh my. That's sounds dangerous," Penny said.

"Arthur loves dangerous cases. Since then, he and Poppy have been an item," Marge said with a grin. "I love your show, are you going to keep doing it?"

"I may retire one day. But for now, I'm happy. I work for about four hours a day, then drive Jim crazy the rest of the day. He's so easy-going and considerate. I guess that's what I love about him."

"Sounds like you have a good marriage," Marge said.

"We do. I think I'll keep him," she laughed as Poppy came back.

"I'm all set for this thing," Poppy said holding up her name badge. "But I'm still open for a spa treatment. The real activities here don't start until this evening."

"I'll probably sit with Jim during the speeches. I'm not fond of listening to long-winded people talk, but maybe they'll have some interesting speakers." Penny said.

"From reading the brochure, they have some good people talking. Lots of topics and advice," Poppy said. "They even have office experts who will talk about report filing and logging cases. I'm sure you'll enjoy that, Marge."

"I look forward to it. Anything to make my life easier is welcome," Marge replied.

"Jim's office manager, Lacey will like that," Penny said. "She's always complaining about the men, and the one woman, not getting their reports in. Even though she's right."

"You have a woman investigator?" Poppy asked.

"Yep, she's a former homicide detective for the Vegas police. She had a baby girl and decided to cut back on all the crime she had to investigate. Her husband was a detective also, he works with us now. He got shot on his last case with LVPD and decided he wanted to live to be around for his daughter's wedding. So he joined us also."

"It sounds like a big firm, do they have enough business to keep going?" Marge asked.

"It's Vegas, baby! There's enough minor crimes going on to keep Jim and his crew busy," Penny said happily.

Buck and I came back to the women. "We're all registered now," I said, as I handed Penny a name badge. "You're also registered. You've helped catch enough criminals to qualify. Have you seen Lacey and Mac?"

"No, they must be sight-seeing," Penny replied.

I pulled my cell phone and called her. After a couple rings, she came on. "I'm on vacation, you better not be wanting me to do anything," she spoke loudly. There was a lot of noise behind her.

"Where are you?" I asked.

"We're out front of the hotel, looking at the city. Lots of traffic and people," she said loudly.

"They're taking registrations, if you want to get in on it," I answered.

"We'll be in shortly. Mac is itching to get in the convention. Is Penny nearby?" Lacey asked.

"She's right here, you want to talk to her?"

"No, we'll be in shortly, it's smelly out here with car exhaust," she said and hung up.

I looked at Penny and said, "Lacey wants to talk to you when she comes in."

"Probably has to do with Jessie. I offered to watch her while Mac and Lacey were in the convention."

"That was nice," I replied. "Maybe we can let Jessie watch Willy, too." Penny agreed.

Doyle came up and smiled at Poppy and Marge. "Are you going to register, Marge? You're my office manager and they have activities for you."

"I'll go take care of that now," she said and went off to the tables.

"Well, this should be an interesting weekend," Doyle said.

"Maybe you'll learn something, Jim," Buck said with a big grin.

"He needs a lecture on napping and avoiding work," Penny added.

"Hey, are you going to start that again? I do work. I started the firm on my own and look how big it's grown."

"Yes, sweetie. You are the Trump of investigating."

"Herman Trump," Buck added.

"I don't need to be abused, I can do that to myself. I'm going to get lunch if anyone wants to follow, my treat."

We were heading to the main lobby again when Lacey, Mac, and Jessie came in. Jessie came bouncing over and latched on to Penny. "Grandma Penny, are you going to take care of me while mom and dad go play detectives?"

"I will, dear. Are you interested in a spa?" Penny asked.

"What's a spa?" Jessie asked.

"Oh, you'll have fun," Poppy said to her. "You get to put mud on your face."

Jessie's eye widened and she giggled.

Penny laughed and introduced Lacey, Mac and Jessie to everyone. Marge came forward to Lacey and said, "I'm the office manager for Doyle and Drew Investigations, we need to talk."

**

Chapter 11

Marge took Lacey and Mac to the registration table as Penny was holding Jessie's hand.

"You and your cavemen can go beat on your chests and get your convention started," Penny said to me. "I saw that they have booths set up with crime-fighting toys you may like."

"I promise not to spend too much money, but I'm hungry, we need to eat first." I turned to everyone still nearby and said, "We can go eat and come back here to explore all the vendors."

"I'm for that," Doyle said.

"I understand you have a partner?" I asked Doyle.

"Yep, Oscar Drew. He's off somewhere in the city and said he'd be here soon," Doyle responded.

Private Eye Murders

Deacon came up and said, "They have great stuff in the vendor areas. Surveillance equipment, listening devices and video equipment. We could really do the job with that stuff. Hey, Doyle, how are you feeling this morning?"

"Good, Deacon, you were enjoying the club. How's your head?"

"Not as bad as Trapper's is. I managed to steer him to registration," Deacon said with a grin.

"Enough talk, food awaits," I called out and headed to the lobby. Everyone followed and we were going to where the restaurants were, when Bernie Longmire came in off an elevator with Gus Mackie.

"Hey, Bernie, Gus, glad you could get here," I said.

"We're just going to register. Your team knows how to party. Too bad you weren't there." Gus said.

"I was getting my rest for today. Us old people need to pace ourselves."

"Hell, I'm not much younger than you and I still can party," Gus said.

"It's all about the desire to party. I gave that up long ago," I said.

"At my insistence," Penny added.

"Have you registered yet?" I asked.

"Just going to do that now," Gus replied.

"We'll wait for you here. We're going to get some lunch, if you want to go with us?" I offered.

Gus looked at Bernie, "Don't ask me, Gus. It's up to you," Bernie said.

"Okay, we'll be right back." Gus and Bernie went off. I knew Bernie didn't have to register, he was a speaker.

We waited for them to come back and made small talk about our firms. Gus and Bernie finally arrived and just as we were getting ready to go eat, there was a blood-curdling scream.

Bernie turned in the direction of the scream and was gone. He was fast for a man his size. He moved down a hallway along the front of the hotel and I could see him stop beside two women. We all rushed down to where they stood looking into an open elevator. There was a man on the floor in a pool of blood. Penny took Jessie down the hallway to keep her from seeing the body.

At first I wondered if this was one of those mystery murder plays they set up for the detectives, but it looked too real. Bernie had entered the elevator and was leaning down to the man.

He looked back and said, "He's dead." He stood and took out his cell phone and made a call.

People were starting to gather, so Doyle and I were moving them back. Our group had moved away from the scene as Bernie was talking to the two women who discovered the body. They looked totally distressed.

Buck and Mac joined us in keeping people away until more police arrived, along with the ME and forensics. They taped off the area and closed down the hallway around the elevator. I took my people to the edge of the tape and watched Bernie talking to one other detective.

"Bernie's with Homicide, so he'll probably take lead," Gus said to me. "Not a good place to have a murder. A convention of P.I.s all wanting to solve the case."

I looked around and saw a large number of men watching the scene, most likely from the convention. Bernie came over to us.

"He was shot in his forehead. Blood splatter all over the elevator car. The perp had to have been covered in it. I sent men up to the floors above to see if they can find the perp or witnesses."

"Have you determined who the vic was?" Doyle asked.

"He had ID, but I can't talk about that until we notify the next of kin," Bernie replied.

"Was he an investigator?" I asked.

"I can say he was. According to his name badge, he signed up just prior to the shooting. He was from Toledo," Bernie said. "If it was someone he wronged during an investigation he performed, then they either followed him here, or lives here."

"It would be strange that someone followed him from Toledo to kill him," Gus said. "Why not do it down there?"

Bernie grinned at Gus and said, "True, Gus. Now I have to get back to my investigation. All of you may as well go eat, nothing you can do here."

Penny said to me, "You're going to try and solve this, aren't you?"

"It's in capable hands, I'll let Bernie work the case. Besides, I said we were going to relax this weekend," I said. "For the last time, let's go eat."

I turned and left the area, followed by Penny with Jessie and the rest of our group. I looked back and Doyle was talking to Gus. That peaked my curiosity. I stopped, Penny nearly running into me.

"We're not going to get food, are we?" Penny asked.

I took out my charge card, handed it to her, and said, "Take everyone to eat. I need to see what Doyle and Gus are up to. I'll join you later."

Penny looked back at Marge, Poppy, Lacey and Mac. "Okay, let's go, troops."

Deacon and Buck stood waiting for me to make a move. "Aren't you going to eat?" I asked them.

"And let you have all the fun? Lead on," Deacon said.

I went back to Doyle and Gus; they turned to us as we came up. "What's up?" I asked.

"Aren't you a bit curious?" Doyle asked.

"I'm here to relax and learn. Bernie's in charge and I'm sure he'll figure it out," I replied.

Gus laughed and said, "Bernie is an excellent detective. Yes, he'll figure it out, but I like to watch him work. For me, it's an on the job experience with him. I don't have a crew to keep track of like you and Doyle. So I'm hanging around."

Private Eye Murders

I grinned and realized he was right. I did have my people to keep track of, but I needed to let them do their thing as I went about my business. That may be this murder. Okay, I'm going to have to turn them loose and see what my new crime fighting friends were going to do.

Bernie came over to us. "I hope you guys aren't plotting to work this? Too many P.I.s will spoil the investigation."

"Bernie, more eyes on the case can help," Gus told his friend.

"Well then, spread out and find a witness, or better yet, the perp. He has to be nearby, probably watching us."

"Maybe he could be a rival investigator, wanting to get rid of the competition," I said.

Bernie grinned and said, "Then go find him."

**

Chapter 12

"Shall we check on our victim's registration to see if he came with anyone?" Doyle said.

"Who are we asking for? We don't even know his name," I said.

Bernie cleared his throat and said quietly, "If I can trust you to keep this under wraps, his name was Klein. Have a nice day," he grinned and walked back to the crime scene.

"There's a lead," Gus offered and went back to the convention's registration table, followed by us.

"May I help you gentlemen?" asked a woman sitting at the table. "Do you wish to register?"

Gus spoke first, "No, we're already registered. We just need some information about an investigator from Toledo, named Klein. He's already registered."

Private Eye Murders

The woman looked at her sign-in sheet and said, "There is one Klein from Toledo, and yes, he's registered. What do you need to know?"

"Was he with anyone else?" Doyle asked.

She looked at the sheet again and said, "No, he signed in as a single. He's the only person from Toledo."

I thought this was going to be more work. A man alone in a place full of investigators, murdered, with no one to claim him as a friend or associate. We thanked the woman and moved away so more people could sign in.

"Well, we have no one to question. Let's look him up and see if he has a firm in Toledo that we can talk to," Gus said.

"What about the convention?" I asked. "Are we working this case or letting Bernie handle it?"

"Would you be able to let it go? A man is murdered in an elevator, I'm curious," Doyle said. "But then, that's the former cop in me. I have to find out who did this and why."

"Okay, so you're on the case?" Buck spoke from behind me. I looked back at him and grinned.

"You can count me out," Deacon said. "I came to enjoy the convention and not solve a murder. I'm going to find Trapper and explore the vendors." He turned and went into the ballroom.

"He's right, I think I'll follow him and explore the vendors too," Buck said and went after Deacon.

I looked back at Doyle and Gus, "Well, that leaves us to do this."

"If it were any other homicide detective, besides Bernie, they'd tell us to keep our noses out of this," Gus said. "Bernie likes to make things easy for him. So he won't mind us snooping around."

"When the woman was looking for Klein's sign-in, I glanced at the registration and Klein was listed in room 526. We could go snoop around his room," Gus said.

"I'm sure the police are already checking the room, but it doesn't hurt to go see," I said.

"Well, we can't take that elevator," Doyle said looking at the crime scene. "There's another couple around the corner."

We went to the elevators and were waiting when a man came up. "Art, what's up?" the man said.

"Hey, Oscar, you made it. What kept you?" Doyle asked.

"A cheating husband, but I got the goods on him," Oscar replied with a grin.

Doyle introduced his partner to us and we all shook hands.

"What's up, as I said?" Oscar asked again.

"There was a murder around the corner from here. We're doing some investigating," Doyle replied.

"Murder? I didn't come here spending six hundred dollars to investigate a murder. I'm going to sign in and enjoy the convention. I have a few friends that I want to catch up with." Oscar said with a grin.

"Go enjoy, Oscar. We have it in hand and if we don't, we'll join you in the ballroom," Doyle said. Oscar said his goodbyes and left as the elevator opened. We waited for people to get off and then got on. Doyle hit the button for the fifth floor and we waited as the car rose.

"I'm on the fifth floor," I said. "I hope the killer isn't going to be hanging around my floor. That won't make my wife happy."

"I'm surprised Poppy didn't want to join us. She loves a good investigation," Doyle said.

"I heard her and my wife talking about a spa treatment. I'm sure your girlfriend will appreciate that more than a murder."

"Very true. Besides we have enough people investigating this," Doyle said. "We don't want this to become a circus."

The doors opened on the fifth floor and we got off. There were police already at the open door of the victim. We walked down the hallway to the cops and stood outside the room.

"Doyle, what are you doing here?" came a voice from in the room. Doyle laughed as the man came out.

"Harold, did they send you to investigate this murder?" Doyle asked the man.

"I was called in to help. They didn't want all you private eyes to screw up the case." The man looked at us and said, "Did you bring your fan club?"

"Guys, this is detective Harold Brunner, a hold-over from an ancient squad." Doyle shook the man's hand. "Harold, this is Gus Mackie and Jim Richards, both owners of investigating firms."

"Richards, you're from Vegas. I remember you from here years ago. Gus, I know you're friends with Longmire," he said. "You run with an exclusive crowd, Doyle."

"Only the best, Harold. What's up in the room?"

"Doyle, you know I can't share that," Harold said.

"I'm not asking for any national secrets, just a bone as to who this guy was."

"Okay, keep this quiet. He was nothing, no secrets, no evidence. Nothing. He left clothes, ugly clothes, but nothing else. The guy was a plain ordinary man."

"Harold, private eyes all have secrets. There wasn't anything in his belongings? No personal letters, threats, love letters?" Doyle asked, surprised.

"Sorry, Doyle, there was nothing. We're about finished, if you do it quietly, I'll leave the door unlocked." Harold turned and went back to the room.

"This is disappointing. The guy comes here and is shot in the head by what looks like a professional hit. He had to have had something that someone wanted. I don't trust Harold, he's old school and we're not real friendly. I'm sure if there was anything important in this room, it will be removed."

We stood back and watched the four men tearing through the room, then come out. Harold closed the door and smiled at Doyle. He went down the hall with his men and left.

Doyle went to the door and gave it a push, it opened. "I doubt we'll find anything, but let's give it a go."

We went in and stood looking around at the mess left by Harold and his crew. The couch was pulled apart, the pillows on the floor and drawers in the desk pulled out, contents strewn.

"I'll take the bedroom," I said, followed by Gus. We went through the room, searching the closet and looking under the bed mattresses. "I don't know if they found anything, but we have to be clever," I said as I bent over to look under the pulled out dresser drawer. I saw it.

"Doyle," I called to him. He came in and over to me as I pulled the envelope taped under the drawer.

He looked at the envelope in my hands and said, "Richards, how would you like to join my firm?"

**

Chapter 13

I opened the envelope and took out a group of photos. We glanced through them quickly as they were pretty explicit photos of a man and woman having sex.

"Well, Klein followed cheating spouses, too," I said.

"But who are they?" Gus asked.

"I'm sure I'll find that out," came a voice from the doorway. It was Bernie. "I figured you would find something that Harold couldn't," he said, coming over to us, reaching for the photos.

"Can we keep one, Bernie?" Gus asked.

"You know better than that, Gus. This is evidence," he smiled and dropped one photo. "Oops, I'll let you pick that up - after I leave," He grinned and left the bedroom.

Gus bent down and recovered the photo. The image only showed the faces close up, not one of them having sex. "Well, we can at least identify them."

Doyle took the photo and studied it. "It looks like a motel room, but how did Klein get these shots from all the angles I saw in the other photos?"

"Yeah, it was almost like he was in the room," I offered.

"Maybe the couple wanted a memory album made. So Klein was hired to photograph them doing it," Gus said with a laugh.

"He may have had multiple cameras set up. I have tiny cameras watching the doors to my office," Doyle said.

"That would mean that he knew the couple was going to be in this particular room," I said.

"It could have been a room they used often, Klein was watching them and knew they'd be back." Doyle looked at the back of the photo and could see a watermark. "This was taken last week according to the time stamp."

"Whatever, why did he bring the photos to the convention and hide them? He had to know that someone here wanted these photos and maybe he was blackmailing that person," I guessed.

"That's very possible, and a good reason for killing him. But why kill him before getting the photos back?" Gus asked.

"Maybe the killer hadn't gotten around to searching the room since the cops were here," I said.

"Why kill him, then let the cops find the photos? It doesn't make sense," Gus wondered.

They heard someone in the main room and rushed out to see who it was. As they came out of the bedroom, they found a man standing in the open doorway.

"Excuse me, is this Jerry Klein's room?" he asked.

"It is, and you are?" Doyle asked him.

"Mike Day, I'm Jerry's associate."

"If you are here to see him, then I'm thinking you haven't heard the news," Doyle said, coming up to the man.

"What news?" he asked.

"Mr. Day, your associate has been murdered," Doyle said unceremoniously.

"What!" Day cried out. He seemed more surprised than upset. I wondered if he had an idea that Klein was a target. "When, where?"

"About two hours ago, in an elevator. He was shot in the head."

"Are you the police?" he asked.

"Private investigators, helping the police. Are you also an investigator?" Doyle asked.

"I am. I was Jerry's partner in our firm. We had a good amount of business, mostly spousal cases."

"Do you know anything about this?" Doyle held up the photo, but didn't let Day handle it. Day got his face up close and squinted.

"Nope, don't know them. Is this something Jerry was involved in?"

"This and a few other photos were hidden together in this room. We think it may have been a good reason for his murder."

"Where are the other photos?" Day asked.

"The police have them. We managed to secure this one for our investigation. Was Klein involved in any recent spousal cases? Ones you may have only heard about but weren't involved in?"

"I don't know, Jerry wasn't very open about his cases. He'd take on ones without consulting me. I'll be honest, I think he had an agenda that wasn't totally legal. That photo may be part of one of those."

"Did he have any enemies?" Gus asked.

"A few. He pissed off a number of husbands who he caught being unfaithful. It's an unpleasant fact of the job."

I had to agree. I've been threatened by a few irate husbands that our firm had exposed.

"Excuse me, but I have people waiting for me. I'm shocked to hear this disturbing news. Thank you for telling me." He turned and left the room. We watched him go.

"I think we need to check on this Day guy," I said. "Maybe he came here to get the photos, figuring the police wouldn't find them."

"Good point. I'll call Bernie and have Day checked on," Gus said. He went off to make the call.

"I'm sure Bernie will be happy to have this tidbit," I said.

We waited until Gus came back. "Bernie thanked us for this info. He's going to run a check on Klein and see who worked with him. If Day isn't a partner, then he'll pull him in."

"If Day isn't already running now, since the photos were found," I said. "Let's check with the registration lady and see what room Day is in."

"I'm for that," Doyle smiled and we left the room.

In the elevator going down, my cell phone buzzed. I looked at the caller ID and saw it was Penny. "Hey, babe, what's up?" I asked.

I didn't put it on speaker, so she spoke in my ear. "I'm taking Poppy, Marge and Jessie to the spa. Have you caught your killer yet?"

"Not yet, so be careful out there," I replied.

"No one better interrupt my spa visit. They will die," Penny said with a snarl. I flinched.

"Go have a good time and enjoy your mud pack," I said and hung up.

The elevator door opened and we exited the car. "That was my wife, she's kidnapped your girlfriend and office manager to go get covered in mud," I said as we walked around to the registration table.

"Back again, gentlemen?" the same woman asked us.

"Did another man register from Toledo?" I asked.

"There have been no other men from Toledo signing in. Sorry."

I looked at Doyle and Gus. "He was right there and we didn't know."

"You couldn't have known," Bernie said coming up to us. "I ran Klein's business, he was alone, with no partners. Could you identify this guy again?"

"He wasn't very plain, we could ID him again," Doyle said.

"He's probably left the building, so I'll have you give a description to our artist and send the image out for a BOLO." Bernie pulled his cell phone.

"Don't you hate it when you face the killer and not know it?" I said.

"We still need to identify the people in the photo," Doyle said.

I was watching Bernie on his phone when a uniform officer came running up to him. They talked briefly then Bernie followed the officer.

We were right on Bernie's heels as he went to a men's room off the lobby. We tried to enter but were stopped by the cop. Bernie was in the room for a few minutes then came out.

"We have another murder," he said quietly.

**

Chapter 14

"Gus, I need you to take a look at this man and see if he's the one you saw up in the room." Bernie turned and went back into the men's room. Gus looked at us then followed.

"Well, this is turning into a great vacation for me," I said sarcastically. "I'm glad my wife is enjoying herself."

We waited in silence for Gus to come back. The patrolman who summoned Bernie was guarding the door, letting no one enter. Finally, Gus came out, he was frowning.

"Well?" Doyle asked.

"It was him. Shot in the head just like Klein."

"Then he wasn't the shooter of Klein." I said.

"His pockets were turned inside out like someone was looking for something," Gus said.

"Maybe the killer was looking for the photos, which Day didn't have," Doyle said. "He didn't get to them before we found them."

"Then Day must have known where the photos were, hoping the police wouldn't find them."

"Why didn't Klein just give the photos to Day, why the subterfuge of hiding them?" I asked.

"And who knew that Day was going to collect the photos?" Gus asked.

"Well, now that we have all the questions, we just have to fill in the answers," I said. "Or look for a guy who matches the man in the photo we have. I think he'd like to have the photos back."

"I agree. Shall we walk around and check out faces in the ballroom? We should split up, it would save time," Doyle said and took out the photo. He showed it to us again to familiarize ourselves on the face, and then we agreed to meet back in an hour.

The three of us went into the ballroom and off in different directions. I figured if this guy was here, he must have been a private investigator himself.

I was walking around the middle of the vendor area, trying not to be distracted by all the great items on sale. I suddenly heard my name called out and turned to the voice. It was Trapper.

"I see you decided to join the convention. Couldn't find your killer?" he asked.

"I'm searching for him now. There was a second murder, so the plot thickens."

"You think he may be in this crowd of men who couldn't pass the requirements to become police?" Trapper said with a grin.

"Don't say that too loud, you may not like to be thrown out. Where's Earl and the rest?"

"Somewhere in the crowd. Deacon was drooling over the surveillance equipment last I saw him."

"Well, it shows he cares. Have you found the bathing beauties selling assault rifles?"

"Yep, and got autographs," he said showing me the photos. I laughed.

"Okay, I have a person to find. You can go back to drooling over bathing beauties," I said and walked away, leaving him laughing.

I got all the way to the end of the vendor area and saw Doyle coming around the booths.

"Anything?" he asked.

"Nope, didn't see anyone who even looked like him," I replied.

Doyle's cell phone rang the theme from the movie, 'Jaws' and I smiled. He took it out and went to answer after looking at the caller ID. "It's my girlfriend," he said.

"Hey, Poppy, what's up?" he said and listened. He grinned, mumbled something I couldn't hear, and then hung up. "She's with your wife, the girl and my secretary. They're in the beauty salon getting the full spa treatment. She was just checking on my progress."

"Didn't have much to tell her, did you?" I replied.

Doyle looked past me and said, "Here comes Gus."

I turned and saw Gus coming through the crowd, he wasn't smiling. He came up and said, "I got nothing, how about you two?"

"Same here. No sign of our cheating spouse," I said.

"In all fairness, we don't know if he was the cheater or she was," Doyle added.

"I'll give you that," I said. "She may have hired a hitman to get back the photos before Klein could show them to her husband. Maybe we need to copy the photo of the woman and go around asking if anyone knows her."

"That's not a bad idea. Or we could post it on the wall and leave our number in tiny tear off tabs," Doyle said.

"You joke but that could work. I saw a booth that had copiers, let's go blow the photo up." I went back down the aisle and found the booth with the copiers. "Give me the photo, Doyle."

He handed it to me, and I asked the man at the counter if he could selectively enlarge the woman's face. He asked if we wanted it made into a wanted poster. I gave him the info, my phone number, and he went to work. I had him make fifteen copies and paid him.

"Here's five for each. Let's put them up around the room." We took them around and asked people at the booths if they could put them up. I was happy that they agreed.

We met back in the lobby by the men's room where Day was murdered. The police still had it taped off, and forensics was combing the area.

Bernie came over and asked, "Have you found the killer yet?"

"We aren't going to do all your work," Gus said and handed him a flyer.

"This is the woman?" he asked.

"Yep, we're hoping someone knows her," Doyle said.

My cell phone buzzed, and I took it out. The caller ID said private. I told the men, "Maybe someone who saw the photos." I answered and put it on speaker. Everyone pulled in close to listen.

The voice on the phone said, "You got the photos?"

I paused and then said, "Why?"

"Look, don't mess with this. You don't know who you're dealing with," he said.

"Should I care?" I asked hoping to anger him.

"You will if you don't want to end up in the Detroit River, buster."

I looked at Bernie, he waved his hand like he wanted me to keep going. "Should I be afraid of you and why do you want the photos?"

"Listen, dickhead, you will be afraid and I want the photos. I've already wasted time killing two men to get them. I'll make you number three."

"You'll have to find me first. Unless you feel brave enough to meet me?"

He didn't say anything for a long moment. Then he said, "Time and place. Bring the photos."

"One hour, under the Joe Lewis fist. I could use some cash so bring money." I hung up.

Bernie said, "That's brave of you. I'll have my men stationed around the statue, and you need a vest. This man has killed two others already, not taking chances."

"He shot the other men in the head. Do you have a bullet-proof helmet he can wear?" Doyle mugged.

"Not funny, Doyle. I'll take my chances," I said.

"Why the fist?" Bernie asked.

"It's open, good view from all around for your men."

"Okay. But not a lot of places to hide for you, if it goes bad," Gus said.

"I'll just have to trust the Detroit police," I said.

"Your first mistake," Doyle laughed.

**

Chapter 15

Bernie had rallied four of his best detectives to go around the statue and watch for my visitor. I was fitted for a vest and Doyle gave me some last minute advice. Mostly to keep my head low.

"What do I do when he shows and I don't have the photos?" I asked Bernie.

He thought a moment and asked, "Where did you get the wanted poster made?" I told him about the copier booth. "Take me there," he said.

We went back and Bernie showed his badge and took out the envelope with the photos from an evidence bag. He explained to the man to be careful handling the photos and asked him to make one copy of each. The man in the booth obliged and when he had them copied, he gave them to Bernie in a new envelope. The originals were put back in the bag. Bernie handed the copies to me and I put them in my jacket pocket.

We went out of the ballroom and Bernie gave me last minute instructions. I finally drove out in a rental car with Doyle and Gus on the back floor, hoping to nab our bad guy. I drove down to Hart Plaza where 'The Fist' was located. It was a memorial to boxer Joe Lewis and was a gigantic arm and fist hanging from a pyramid support.

I parked just off the plaza and walked over to the statue. Gus and Doyle got out after I left and causally walked around the plaza. I stood just under the huge fist, thinking the thing would collapse and crush me. That would top off my day.

I had no idea who the detectives were who were watching me, there were a number of people in the plaza so it would be easy to be unseen. I stood watching for a man to approach me, when I saw a boy of about twelve looking like he may have been begging for change.

He finally came up to me and I was ready for him when he asked, "Are you the man with the photos?"

That threw me. "What do you mean?" I asked him.

"Mister, do you have photos?" he replied.

"I do, were you sent to get them?"

"The man told me to get the photos and bring them to him," he said nervously.

"Well, you go back and tell him that he has to get them himself."

"Look, mister, if I don't bring them, he said he'd kill my sister. He has her in his car."

That sent a chill through me. I was wired, so I hope Bernie could hear what the boy said. I looked around wishing someone would give me an answer. I had to hope Bernie would adjust his plan and would have the boy watched as to where he went. I took out the envelope with the pictures and handed them to the boy.

"Listen to me, you refuse to give these to the man until he releases your sister, understand?"

He nodded his head quickly and then ran off. I watched the way he was going, hoping everyone was watching him. I saw Doyle and Gus going in the direction of the boy. I stood there feeling helpless, so I moved in the same direction.

I saw two patrol cars come flying in the parking area and men get out. Then I saw Doyle holding hands with the children coming away from the parking area. I guess he figured what was going on.

I went to Doyle and asked, "Did they get him?"

Doyle frowned and said, "After he dumped the girl, he sped out. They put a BOLO on the car, but he's gone."

I looked down at the boy and said, "You did good. But next time, stay away from strangers."

Bernie came up and said, "I'll take the children. We'll need to get their parents in and then ask the boy about the man. At least no one was hurt."

Bernie bent down and smiled at the children asking if they'd like a ride in a police car. They both smiled and nodded. "Gus, come with me to help with them," Bernie asked. The four of them went off and I turned to Doyle.

"Did you get a look at the car?" I asked.

Private Eye Murders

"Late model Chevy Impala, dark blue, about 1999. It should be easy to spot. I'm sure he's going to think he got the only photos, he couldn't know we had them copied so quickly." He looked at me and smiled. "Don't you love technology?"

"Too bad we didn't have a tracker to put on the photos. Did you get a look at the man?"

"He had tinted windows, so it wasn't easy to see him. Maybe the kid will give a better description," Doyle said.

"This guy is a creep, to use children to do his dirty work. I hope they find him quickly."

My cell phone buzzed and I took it out. The caller ID said private, so I showed it to Doyle then put it on speaker. "Hello," I said.

"Are you still looking for the woman in your flyers?" came a male voice.

"We are. Do you know her?" I asked.

"I do, but it's going to cost you for the name."

"Why the hell does everyone put a price on information?" Doyle said loudly.

The voice spoke again, "Hey, loudmouth, I have to make a living. Now if you want the name, meet me in front of the MGM Grand, I'll have on a white sports coat. I think ten grand would do nicely."

"Well, if you want that kind of money you'll have to give us an hour," I said.

"Fine, be there." He hung up.

"I think we need to talk to Bernie," I said. "If this guy knows the woman, then there must be others. If they arrest him, they'll find out where he's from, which will give us a start."

"Let's go back to the hotel and get ready. Do you have ten grand on you?" Doyle said with a grin.

"I think I'd rather beat the info out of him than give him any money," I responded.

"I'm with you there." We went to the rental car and drove back to the hotel. "I'm sure Gus will call when he's done helping with the children," Doyle said on the way.

"This all seems like a case of blackmail of someone powerful. It has to be to go to all this trouble. Two murders and mysterious dealings with the killer and the photos. I wonder if we can get the woman's face on the six o'clock news. That might stir something up."

"Actually, that's not a bad idea. They could say that she's missing and wanted in connection with two murders. Not a lie, but it all goes together. Let's talk to Bernie and see what can be done."

We arrived back at the hotel and I parked. We went around to the front lobby and watched for a man in a white jacket. Doyle laughed when he saw the man. I followed him out the doors and over to the man.

Doyle grabbed him by the collar and swung him to the concrete short wall. "Mickey, long time no see," Doyle growled. "Jim, meet Mickey 'Mouse' Mahaffey. Con man and extortionist."

**

Chapter 16

"Mickey, are you scamming us about the woman in the photo?" Doyle asked, twisting Mickey's arm. He was wincing in pain as Doyle pushed the black man to sit down on a bench. "Talk Mickey, or I'll turn you over to the police for extorting money from us for info."

"Hey, Doyle, I have the info, I just need a little cash to live on," the man said.

"You're not an investigator, how'd you get in to see the flyers?"

"I got a friend, he's a private dick. I was with him. I knew the bitch in the photo, she's a hooker, came up from Toledo to get away from some bad guys. She got involved with more bad guys up here. The bitch just can't stay out of trouble."

"What's her name, Mickey?"

"You got the money?" he responded. Doyle whacked him in the head. "Hey, I'm not asking for much."

I took out a twenty from my pocket and held it out to him. He reached for it and I pulled back. "First, the name," I said.

"Damn. Okay, bitch's name is Corletta Kemper. Lives off Brush Street, that's all I know. She be a high priced ho, works through an escort service." Mickey looked at the twenty and I gave it to him. "Am I free to go now?"

"If I find you lied to us, I'll track you down. Understand?" Doyle snarled in his face.

"Anything you say, Doyle, I don't want to see you again," he said, then jumped up and ran.

"Do you believe him?" I asked.

"Yeah, Mickey's a scum, but he's honest. He works as a snitch for a number of detectives. Let's see what Gus is up to," he said and pulled his phone. He dialed the number and Gus answered. "Gus, is Bernie nearby?"

Gus put Bernie on his phone and Doyle said, "Got some info for you, the woman in the photo is Corletta Kemper, high priced hooker lives around Brush. If you find out who she is, I'd appreciate a courtesy reply." Doyle listened and then hung up.

"Well, we've done our civic duty to law enforcement. Shall we go enjoy the convention?"

"I'm all for that," I said and we went into the building and to the ballroom. I saw Lacey and Mac with Buck at the entrance and went to them.

"Lacey, you didn't want to go to the spa?" I asked her.

"Do I look like I need a spa treatment? I need a whole new face," she replied.

Mac said, "Baby, you're beautiful to me without a spa treatment."

"That's why I keep you around, to boost my morale," she said, looking back at me. "Is Jessie still with Penny?"

"I think I saw Jessie at the blackjack table," I said joking. Lacey gave me a dirty look and I said, "She's with Penny in the spa getting the works. She's doing fine."

"She better be. Bad enough you grandparents spoil her, but don't even get her into gambling," Lacey said.

"I don't mind Jessie calling me Grandpa Jim, but you don't need to do it," I warned her.

Trapper and Earl came out the doors and over to us. "Are you going in?" Trapper asked.

I said, "Doyle and I are going to check out the vendors, finally."

"Lots of good stuff," Earl said and showed me his pile of brochures. He had a number of gun related brochures, which was so Earl. "I may change my weapon of choice. I saw a great Sig Sauer P224 Extreme, that I may get. Small, yet powerful."

"Did you see anything useful for solving crimes?" I asked.

"Oh sure, good surveillance equipment," Earl said. "We can always use that. There were a number of items of great covert spying equipment that would help us. Go take a look."

"I will, now that our case has stalled, but only temporarily," I said. I looked at Doyle and asked, "Shall we go spend some money?"

We went into the ballroom and wandered the booths. "Are you happy being a P.I. now, away from being a cop?" I asked Doyle, as we checked out the gadgets to help fight crime.

"I spent ten years on the FBI terrorist task force and ten years as a cop, working my way up to homicide detective. All I've known is law enforcement. I have no other skills other than killing people for the government and arresting people for the city. I guess the natural progression from homicide is my own business chasing cheating spouses," he laughed.

"Don't feel bad. I'm in Vegas and the most we do is chase spouses. I've been lucky to have a few great cases of terrorism, but it's not always glamorous." I picked up a brochure about micro-sized listening devices.

"Even in the FBI, I handled a lot of cases that any city cop could have done. Although the serial killer cases were interesting. This blackmail case has my blood pumping. Who could be the victims and who are the killers. Murder was a big part of being a homicide cop in Detroit, but most killings were gang related. So they were easily solved. I love a good case that takes deduction and reasoning to solve."

"Like Sherlock Holmes did. I caught the reference to your name."

Doyle laughed and said, "Blame my father, he loved Holmes. He believed we were related to Sir Arthur Conan Doyle, but could never prove it."

"Does it matter? You carry on the lineage of detectives with the name."

"Very true," he said as his phone played Jaws. He looked at the caller ID, it said private. He said hello and listened, then hung up.

"That was Bernie, they tracked down Corletta and found her dead. This is getting deeper in doggie-doo."

When he said that I thought about Willy still up in the room. "Hey, I need to check on something, care to join me?"

"Sure. What's up?" he asked.

"You'll see," I said and we went out to the elevators.

"We're going to your room to rescue your dog, right?" he said with a grin as we went up.

"You are a regular Sherlock Holmes," I laughed.

We got off on the fifth floor and went to my room. I looked over to the room where Klein was staying. It was still taped over by the police. We entered my room and I went to let Willy out of the bathroom. He shot out and over to Doyle.

"Wow that is one cute dog. He's a toy Yorkie, right?" he said and picked up Willy, who didn't seem to mind.

I got Willy's doggie bag and took him from Doyle. I put him in the bag and said, "I think Willy needs to get out of the room."

"Maybe he can track our killer," Doyle said with a laugh.

"I wouldn't put it past him." We left the room and I looked again to the room where Klein was staying. The tape was pulled down and the door was opened. I pointed this to Doyle and we went to the room.

Doyle took out his Sig and peeked around the corner. He saw a woman in the room.

**

Chapter 17

Doyle quietly moved around the door as the woman went into the bedroom. We both moved over to the bedroom door and saw the woman on her knees looking under the dresser drawer.

"Too late, we already got the envelope," Doyle said.

The woman came up quickly and banged her head on the drawer. "Damn it," she cursed, rubbed her head and stood.

We entered the room, Doyle still training his Sig on the woman. "Who are you and what are you doing here?"

She didn't say anything. Doyle looked to me and said, "Call Longmire and have him come and get her."

"Wait," she finally spoke. "I just came to get the photos that Jerry hid here. He asked me to get them and move them to a safe place."

"You knew Jerry Klein?" I asked.

She paused, then said, "He's my husband."

That surprised us, but we had no idea that he was married. "When did you last talk to him?" Doyle asked.

"Last night, around eleven. He said that he hid the envelope under the dresser drawer and I was to take it away. He was afraid someone would find it."

"Did you know what was in the envelope?" I asked.

Private Eye Murders

"Photos, but he said not to look inside."

"Do you know where your husband is right now?" Doyle asked.

"He said he was going to lay low for a while until he made contact with the person wanting the photos. I have no idea where he is now."

Doyle put his weapon away, went to her and pulled her gently to the bed and had her sit. "Mrs. Klein, I have bad news for you. Your husband was murdered earlier today."

The woman's expression went to shock. She burst out crying as I went to Doyle pulling him away from the woman and taking him aside.

"I was thinking, why didn't she wonder about the crime scene tape on the door and why wait so long to come up from Toledo since she talked to him last night. It's only an hour away. Something's fishy here," I said.

We looked back at the woman and she was standing, holding a gun on us. "Gentlemen, please move aside." She said as she backed to the door. She got to the door when she gave a surprised expression. Gus was behind her with his gun in her back.

"Don't move fast or I'll give you a nice hole in your back," he said as Doyle rushed to her and took the gun. He looked at it and saw it was a Walther PPK 9mm, same bullet size that murdered Klein and Day from what he saw.

"Not upset that your husband is dead now, are you?" Doyle asked.

"Screw you," she said as Doyle spun her around and put one of his plastic zip cuffs on her wrists.

"Gus, call Bernie and have him come get this woman," Doyle told him. He looked at me and said, "This is getting complicated. But now we have a live suspect."

Doyle took her to the couch in the living area and pushed her down. "You know, cupcake, we might have believed you if you hadn't pulled the gun. Did you think you could get away?"

"Screw you," was all she said again.

"Nasty, isn't she?" I said.

Private Eye Murders

About ten minutes later, Bernie showed up and had two officers take the woman away. He questioned us and we told him everything. We gave him the gun and he said he'd have ballistics run it. He gave us his thanks and left.

I turned to Gus and asked, "How did you find us here?"

"I saw you and Doyle get on the elevator and watched it go up to five, your floor, Jim. I had to wait for a crowd of people getting on and off the other elevator since the police still had the one elevator taped off. I finally came up and saw the open door and torn crime scene tape and stood out here listening to what was going on. She backed right into me."

"I don't think she would have shot us, but she might have gotten away," Doyle said. "I wonder what her story is?" Doyle said.

"Well, she's not the woman in the photos. Maybe she's married to the man in the photos and wanted them for a divorce," I was guessing.

"That's good. It may explain why she wanted the photos. She may have lied about

Klein being her husband and hired Klein to get evidence of her real husband's affair, and Klein told her he had the photos. I hope Bernie can get something out of her."

I looked down and realized I still had Willy in his bag. "I need to take my dog out and feed him. Care to join me or go exploring on your own?"

"I think I'd like to go in and see what Bernie can get out of the woman. I'll call you if anything develops," Doyle said and we left the room.

We parted at the lobby, Gus went with Doyle, and I stood wondering where I could get some dog food. I heard a voice behind me saying, "What are you doing with that dog, mister?" I turned to find Penny and Jessie standing behind me.

"I was just wondering how I was going to feed him. Do you have some dog food on you?" I asked.

"As a matter of fact, I do." She opened her purse and took out a pouch of dry dog food. "Let's go outside and feed him there. Jessie, would you like to feed Willy?"

The girl nodded her head and I gave her the bag with the dog in it. We went to the exit and out to the front of the hotel. We went off the side and Penny opened a pocket on Willy's bag and took out a leash. She clipped him to it and handed Jessie the leash as Penny put the dry food in a small bowl from another pocket. Willy went at it.

"So, where are Marge and Poppy?" I asked.

"They went to eat after Poppy called Doyle. I heard you guys caught a femme fatale committing a crime."

"You could say that. She's in police custody and they're beating her to talk," I said.

"What?" Jessie said. "Do the police beat people?"

"No, dear. Your grandpa was trying to be funny. Police don't beat people," Penny explained.

"Not publicly," I whispered to my wife. She whacked me on the shoulder. Willy finished up his food and I said that we should take a walk to let Willy do his thing.

We walked down the front of the hotel and around the side, where Willy obligingly took a dump. I pulled one of the plastic bags from the pocket of the dog bag and scooped up the mess. I put it in another pocket for his little presents to be emptied later.

"Now what shall we do?" Penny asked.

"Now that Willy has eaten, we could go get dinner," I answered.

"I'm good with that. All those spa treatments made me hungry." She replied.

I looked at Jessie and said, "Did you like the spa?"

"Sure," she bubbled, "I liked the mud bath."

**

Chapter 18

We went to the rental car and headed to a nearby restaurant. I called Lacey and told her we were taking Jessie for dinner. She said she and Mac were going to a show in the showroom. Jessie was in the back seat playing with Willy as I drove and said to Penny, "Are you going to join me for the lectures?"

"I'll sit through one, then decide if I want to hear more," she replied.

"They have an actor, to be named later, who plays a detective on TV. He's going to speak on the way TV glamorizes the business. Like he really knows."

"I've probably interviewed him on my show. They all live in a fantasy world. Although I enjoyed Hill Street Blues when it was on. That seemed real."

"My life as a private investigator has been exciting, most of the time. When we have those big cases that threaten humans."

"Which are few and far between. You've been lucky to be in a city that has enough nut cases that want to kill many people. I'm not talking about serial killers. Terrorists have the corner on mass murders."

I pulled into a restaurant that was new. I hoped it was good. We were finally sitting in the dining area as my phone rang.

"Really? During dinner," Penny said. "That better be important."

"All my calls are important," I said as I looked at the caller ID. "Why am I getting all these private numbers?" I answered. I didn't put it on speaker because I didn't want Jessie to hear. It was Doyle. "What's up?" I asked.

"The fake wife was just that, fake. Her real husband is a big shot in the Detroit underworld. She wouldn't give much information, but her driver's license gave her away. She's a tough one and had a number of high priced lawyers who came in to get her released. Her husband showed up also and made a big fuss. Bernie took him aside and showed him the photos, he shut up quickly. Since the photos are evidence, they aren't being released. So Mr. Big Shot tucked his tail and took his wife home. I imagine they'll find her floating in the river."

"Well, if he does anything, he'll be the first to be looked at. I imagine he knows the ropes."

"True. We still don't know who murdered Klein and Day and why. The mobster didn't know about the photos so he wouldn't have hired the hitman. The wife had no reason to murder if she hired Klein to take the photos. That's why she was in the room looking for the photos."

"Well, it's late and there are the opening ceremonies for the convention tonight. So, I'm off the case for now," I said.

"I'll see you in the ballroom for the opening. I'll call when I get there," Doyle said and hung up.

"Who was that, sweetie?" Penny asked after I put my phone away.

"Doyle. Filling me in on the progress of the case," I replied.

"So you've turned it into a case? Who's paying you for this?"

"No one, it's just an exercise in investigating."

"Did the convention people set this up as an exercise?" she asked.

"No, of course not. It just happened to be at the convention, unfortunately for the victims.

"Do you think you can solve it before the convention ends? Or will we end up staying over again?"

"If we don't figure out who the hitman is, we'll still leave Monday morning. I want to get back to my office in Vegas."

"Is your couch calling you to nap?" Penny said with a giggle.

"No, we are needed to serve the community. I'm sure the LVPD is going crazy trying to solve their cases without us around."

"You keep telling yourself that," Penny said as our food came.

We enjoyed the meal, it was very good. I paid and we drove back to the hotel.

We took Jessie back to Lacey in their room. They told us all about the show they saw then Penny and I went back to our room to change our clothes. We went back down to the ballroom and went in. The room was busy with people and tables that were decorated and starting to fill, then I saw Trapper and he came over.

"Do we need to listen to the opening speeches?" he asked.

"Will, we're here, may as well enjoy the whole thing. Have you seen Earl, Deacon and Buck?"

"They're seated over there at a table, and are holding seats for you and Penny. Lacey, Jessie and Mac are at another table with people he knows," Trapper said and moved through the crowd to the table, with us following him.

We sat as the lights dimmed and the show began. The chairman of the convention, Bert Yarrow, talked about the mission of the convention. He did well. Then each of the four principal organizers spoke. They finally introduced Greg Jackson, actor in "Detroit P.I." TV show. He was good, giving credit to the many investigators in the city for help to make his role realistic.

Penny was snorting when he built up the part of his character. "Stop that," I scolded.

"He's so full of himself. I live with you and watch your team and he doesn't represent what actual investigators are about," she said. A few people around us agreed with her. Of course, they all knew who she was.

The ceremony came to an end and the open bars opened up. My men all headed to the nearest one, except Buck, who didn't drink.

"Buck, I'm sure they have soda pop in cans. Go enjoy yourself," I said.

He grinned and went away. Penny said in my ear, "You've been a good boy and haven't had a beer in two days. Are you going to go get a couple for us?"

I grinned and kissed her on the cheek. "I'll be right back," I said and went to the bar. On my way, I found Gus and Bernie standing outside the crowd around the bar. "Waiting for an opening?" I asked.

"I should have brought my own. I may do a beer run later," Gus said.

"I'll join you, if I can't get near the bar. These guys are all heavy drinkers."

Bernie laughed and said, "I can have a patrol car pick up a case and deliver it to your room."

"No, it's more fun fighting the crowds. Reminds me of my wasted youth running the bars," I said thinking back. "Anything more about the mobster's wife?"

"Nope, she's gone and hopefully not murdered. Her husband wasn't happy that she hired a P.I. to get the goods on him."

"So he was the man in the photos?" I asked.

"He was and he denied knowing what happened to the hooker and why she was murdered. I'm still going to be watching him."

There was a break in the crowd at the bar so we slipped in. I got four beers for Penny and me, better than trying to get back in. "Where are you sitting?" I asked Gus.

"We got here late so we don't have a table," he replied.

"Follow me, we have room at our table." I turned and went back through the crowd.

**

Chapter 19

My cell phone buzzed, it was Doyle. "You missed the big opening ceremony," I said when I answered.

"I made it back in time to catch the actor bragging. I'm at a table with Marge, Oscar and Poppy. Where are you?"

"On the south side, by the open bar. Gus and Bernie are with us now. We have a big table if you'd like to join us."

"We probably will. The people over here aren't very friendly," he laughed into the phone. "See you shortly."

They arrived and Poppy went straight to sit next to Penny. I was glad that Penny had someone who could keep her company. She and I were comfortable with each other, but we would get bored with nothing new to talk about. Poppy was a breath of fresh air for her.

Everyone was yacking it up and telling stories, having fun with our new friends. Lacey, Jessie and Mac finally joined Buck, Deacon, Earl, Trapper and us so my whole team was there.

The evening finally got late and the ballroom had to be closed. Everybody filed out, most of them probably going to the nightclub. Buck, Earl and Trapper decided to continue partying at the club. Gus said he was going to his room to lounge in the tub and get some rest and Bernie left the hotel. He either was going home or to his precinct, I didn't ask. Poppy invited Penny and Marge to go dancing, so they left us. Doyle, Oscar and I stood alone in the crowd moving out of the room. Oscar said he was going to watch the women to make sure they were all right, which made Doyle and I feel better.

"So, we still don't know who killed our victims. We have a lot of suspects but no leads. There's a quiet little bar in this place, shall we go sit and talk?"

I agreed and we walked out to find the intimate bar overlooking the city. It was a nice quiet place to talk and enjoy a beer or two. We sat near the window looking down on the streets.

"So, to sum it up, Klein is hired by the mobster's wife to catch him cheating," I said. "The photos are hidden while Klein enjoys the convention, but someone wants the photos. Klein refused to give them to the assailant and gets killed. We find the photos and give them to Bernie, but the wife shows up to claim the photos. Her hubby didn't know she hired Klein, and probably will make her life miserable."

"The mobster wouldn't have put a hit out on Klein, he didn't know about the photos. The wife had no reason to kill him, she just wanted the photos. But who was Day and why did he want the photos?" Doyle wondered as he sipped his beer. "This is one big mess."

"Maybe someone else knew about the photos and wanted them to blackmail the mobster. He could have found out from the hooker and killed her to remain anonymous. Either he was Day or someone who hired Day to get the photos. Did Bernie find out anything about Day?"

"Day was a thug who had tons of priors. I'd say you're right about him being hired to get the photos. The wife talked to Klein about the photos and he told her where he hid them, so she knew. But Day had no idea and we stopped him before he could search."

"So we have a mystery man who wanted the photos, possibly for blackmail. Who would benefit from blackmailing the mobster. By the way, what was his name?"

"Lou Saretta, the wife was Loretta." Doyle said.

"Loretta Saretta? That must have been funny to a lot of people in Lou's mob."

"Not if they wanted to live, I'm sure. I'd say someone in Lou's organization wanted to move up and if he could blackmail Lou into stepping down, it could be a reason," Doyle guessed.

"In the old days they would wait until Lou was in a restaurant eating, then go in and blast him with tommy guns."

"Tommy guns? You're showing your age," Doyle laughed.

"That was even before my time. I wasn't born until 1949. Far from the roaring twenties," I defended.

"So, we need to find this blackmailer. But we'd have to talk to Lou about who could do this."

"I'm not keen on talking to a mobster. I did that out in Vegas with a very old mob boss in exile. He was decent but I wouldn't push the issue. Lou may want to handle this himself if we inform him about the attempt."

"It would make our case a lot easier," Doyle laughed.

We sat talking about our lives as private investigators. Doyle had much better stories about his past, mine were boring. About an hour later, my cell phone rang just as Doyle's did. I saw it was Penny and answered. "What's up?"

"I need to be bailed out," was her reply. I laughed and asked why. "Poppy took Marge and me to a club on Woodward, where some guy tried to get fresh with Poppy and me, so Oscar stepped in and a fight started. The man had more buddies and they stepped in, which made Poppy and me step in. We all stepped into the mess when the police arrived. So come get me."

I laughed and asked, "What precinct are you in?"

Penny asked someone and then said, "The 38th precinct, wherever that is."

"We'll find it, hang in there," I said and hung up.

Doyle hung up his phone. "Poppy?" I asked.

"Yep, they're in jail," he grinned. "They're in Bernie's precinct, I'll call him to see what he can do." We drank up and went down to my rental car, Doyle talked to Bernie, he said he was in the station already. He told Doyle he'd process them out.

We arrived at the building and went in, Doyle knew it well. He had started there briefly before he moved to his last station.

Poppy, Penny, Marge and Oscar were sitting on a bench in the lobby as we came in. "Oscar, I'm surprised at you. A former officer of the law, getting into a brawl."

"I was defending the women," he replied with a grin. "I found out they could defend themselves better."

Bernie came over and said, "We're letting them go with a warning. They called me in when Oscar explained he was a former cop and knew me. Take them to their rooms, they are a bit drunk."

Doyle and I said we would, and thanked him. We led our inebriated friends out of the building and to the car. They piled into the back seat and I drove back to the hotel. I let them off at the entrance and told Penny to stay with me. Doyle led his crew into the hotel as I went to park.

"I'm surprised at you. You're lucky there weren't any photographers who recognized you. The scandal magazines would love to have a shot of you fighting in a bar."

"I know, but we were helping Oscar who was getting ganged up on," she replied.

I kissed her and said, "That's my little slugger."

**

Chapter 20

We went up to our room and I let Willy out of the bathroom. He bounced around as Penny opened another food pouch for him. She staggered to the bed and plopped down without removing her clothes. I helped her out of them and tucked her into bed. She was purring like a kitten and said, "Goodnight sweet prince."

I got undressed and crawled into the sheets, snuggling up to Penny who was snoring softly. I must have fallen asleep shortly after.

Saturday morning, and the sun coming in the window woke me. I looked at my watch and it was now just past eight. I got up and went to shower, shave and get dressed. Penny was still sprawled out over the bed, sound asleep. I've never seen Penny drink to excess, this was a first. I took out my cell phone and snapped a couple photos of her to remind her of her night.

I called Doyle and asked how his people were doing. "They're all still sleeping. I'm not going to disturb them. They'll all have huge hangovers today," he said with a laugh.

"Penny is still out. I probably should wake her but I think she'd hit me. So, are we going to investigate today?"

"I called Bernie and got the location of Lou Saretta. Couldn't hurt to talk to him. Although Bernie warned me about it. He said Saretta wasn't very friendly about the matter. I got an address of the construction site Saretta is running today. I'll pick you up at the front entrance. Look for a cherry red Dodge Charger, that'll be me." He hung up and I looked in on Penny, she was still asleep. I wrote a note and left it on the desk in the main room, then quietly slipped out.

Doyle was waiting for me and I got in the car. "Nice ride, is it souped-up?"

"Of course, police interceptor package and high performance engine. Not many criminals could out-run it." He started the car and drove out.

We made small talk about our drunken friends and then he pulled into the construction site where a building was being put up. We saw only a few people working since it was Saturday, then saw a big man in a white shirt who probably was Saretta. We exited the car and went to him.

"Mr. Saretta," Doyle called out. The man turned and gave us an unfriendly look.

"You two cops?" he said with a gravelly voice.

"No, private investigators. We'd just like to ask you a few questions, if you don't mind." Doyle said.

"Well, I do mind. I have a building to finish and questions just slow me down."

"We're just trying to find out who may want to blackmail you." That got his attention.

"What do you mean blackmail?" he said coming closer.

"Well, yesterday there were two murders over those photos of you. We think maybe someone else besides your wife wanted the photos."

"Look, the only person who I wouldn't want to see the photos would be my wife. But that's kind of late now that she knows about them. So I don't see how anyone could blackmail me with the photos."

"It's possible since the hooker you were photographed with was also murdered. That puts the suspicion on you for the kill."

He gave us a dirty look, I was ready to run. "I didn't kill no hooker, she was someone I picked up off the street and that's all I know about her. That Indian cop asked me all those questions, so talk to him."

"Can you just give us a name of anyone who'd like to see you out of the way?" Doyle asked.

"Grab a copy of the Detroit phone book, point to anyone. That's who." He turned and walked away.

We stood there as the workers were busy around us. One worker came over and said quickly, "Meet me at Jack's Bar on Chene Street at five." Then he moved away.

I looked at Doyle and said, "Well, we stirred up something." He agreed and we left the site.

On the way back, Doyle said, "There's more to this than Saretta is saying. Hopefully this guy will have some answers."

"It's ten now, we have seven hours before we meet with him. I told my mother we would visit with her, so I think this would be a good opportunity."

"I'll probably just go wander the vendors again, sit in on a few lectures and relax. Bernie is going to give his speech around seven tonight, so we should be finished with our informer by then."

We parted in the lobby and I went to see if Penny was up. She was in front of the TV with Willy as I came in. She gave me a bleary eye and said, "I hurt all over."

I kissed her on the forehead and sat next to her. "It's amazing what alcohol can do for a person's response to a fight. You're lucky you didn't get bruised or a black eye." We sat in quiet for a short while as we watched a show about animals in the wild. Willy would growl at the lions every so often.

"I'm calling my mother and we'll go visit for a short while," I said and pulled my cell phone out. My mother was happy to hear from us and said she'd tell my brother and son. I hung up and looked at Penny. "Think you can force yourself to get dressed?"

She moved Willy and carefully stood. "I'll be ready in thirty." She waddled to the bathroom and closed the door.

Thirty minutes later, almost on the nose, she came out all bright-eyed and ready to go. We left the hotel and I drove up to my mother's home. We visited with my family for about four hours then begged off to go back to the convention. We had a nice time visiting and I said Penny and I would come out one day alone and visit longer.

Penny was quiet the whole time we were there. I'm sure her head was spinning, but she held up. I parked the car at the hotel and we went back into the ballroom. I had Willy in his bag, I didn't feel like taking him to the room. He needed the fresh air.

We wandered around the vendors, Penny found a few of them interesting and she enjoyed collecting brochures. There was an announcement about a lecture that was going to be given by a nationally known private investigator who had a TV show to help find criminals. He was going to talk about his experience tracking men and women on the run.

Penny was trying to keep awake during the lecture, I found it interesting. I felt my cell phone vibrate, I had shut off the sound during the lecture. I saw it was Doyle and answered.

"Are you listening to this guy brag about his captures?" he said.

"Where are you?"

"In the back, with my people. I'm ready to go talk to our supposed snitch, if you are."

"I'll bring Penny and she can bond with Poppy. Is she still suffering?"

"Not as badly as Oscar. Poppy can drink me under the bar, so she's feeling good. See you shortly."

The lecture ended and we went to find Doyle. He had Gus with him now and Penny went to Poppy and gave her a hug. They both looked beat.

**

Chapter 21

"Our first night in town and the women get arrested for brawling," I said. "I would have thought it would have been us men."

Penny gave me a dirty look so I shut up. Doyle came over to me and said, "I'm ready to go, if you are. I asked Gus to join us."

"Good by me, he's close with Bernie and we may need him," I said. I turned to Penny standing next to Poppy and Marge, and said. "We have to go talk to a guy. We should be back in time for Bernie's lecture."

"So, go. I'm used to you rushing out. Maybe Poppy, Marge and I can go get arrested again," she said.

"I'm not bailing you out this time, so don't commit any felonies." I kissed her and told Doyle to leave quickly.

Doyle asked Oscar to entertain the women and keep them out of trouble. "I'll try, but they can overpower me," he replied with a grin.

"Do your best. We won't be gone long," Doyle said, then muttered, "I hope."

We went to my car again, more room for the three of us, and drove out to find Jack's Bar. Gus knew where it was so we found it in no time. I parked on the side and we got out, going to the front door. The place looked to be a hundred years old, and falling apart. It was dark as we entered and it smelled of stale beer and puke. There were about eight people scattered around the room. There was no pool table, the place was too small for one. So three men were playing cards and they were eyeing us.

"We look like cops, they probably are gambling. I hope our man shows up soon, before they escort us out," Doyle said. The front door opened and in came the worker from the site. He motioned us to a table on the front side of the room, so we went over there.

We sat as an overweight woman came and asked what we wanted. We ordered beers and she waddled off. I turned to the man and said, "Who are you?"

"Jake Mallone. I work for Saretta as his right hand man, but that doesn't mean I like him. I heard you asking questions about blackmail. I know what he's not telling you. What's in this for me?"

Doyle sat back and growled, "Here we go again. Wanting money for information. Richards, do you have another twenty."

I smiled and said, "What do you want?"

"Safe passage out of Detroit, a new identity and to be relocated elsewhere. Saretta will kill me if he found out I ratted him out. But I want to see him fail."

"Fail? In what?" Doyle asked.

"That's the info I have, now do we have a deal?"

I looked at Gus, "Do you think Bernie can get the Marshals to put him in Witness protection?"

"I'm sure he can. As long as Saretta is taken down. He runs too many criminal activities in Detroit."

"I want assurances," Mallone said.

Gus took out his cell phone and called Bernie. He explained what we were up to, Bernie said he could arrange it and told us to be careful. Gus nodded to us and put the phone away.

"Okay, what do you know?" I asked him.

He sat back as the woman brought our beers. He grabbed the can and downed it in one swig. I hoped he wouldn't get too drunk before talking to us.

"Mallone, start talking," Doyle said forcefully. "Talk now or I'll call Saretta and tell him you're ratting him out."

That got his attention. "Okay, I'll tell ya. Saretta is planning on running for city council. Just so he can set up his own agenda for his criminal activities. He found out his wife hired the P.I. to catch him, but after the fact. He realized the photos would ruin his chances. So he sent a man to retain the photos. But the cops got to them first. It seems someone else wants to embarrass him so they killed Saretta's man."

"That must have been Day," Doyle said. "So who is this person who wants to ruin Saretta's chances at a seat on the city council?"

Mallone was quiet for too long. "Come on Mallone, finish this off," Doyle insisted.

The man looked at us and said, "I'm not sure. I just know what Saretta was up to. That's all."

I sat back, disappointed. "Okay, who would benefit from keeping Saretta from getting on the council?"

Mallone said, "Harvey Penrod. He's a contender for the seat. But I can't verify that. I do know that Mrs. Saretta is real friendly with Penrod."

"She may have told Penrod about Klein getting the evidence on her husband. He could have set up the attack for the photos," I said. "Loretta said she talked to Klein about where the photos were. The killer didn't know this and tried to force Klein into talking but killed him. Then he cornered Day in the men's room and killed him too."

"Okay, Mallone, go to the 38th precinct and ask for Detective Longmire. He'll set you up with the Marshal services," Gus told the man.

Mallone looked around, stood and left quickly.

"Okay, who's Penrod?" I asked.

"He was part of the former mayor's administration. Before they all got busted for corruption," Doyle said. "He's been laying low trying to rebuild his reputation."

"So he wants to take a run at getting back into the political machine and will try to prevent any opponent from running," Gus said.

"Seems that way, but murder has entered the political arena. We need to talk to Penrod," Doyle said.

"Why don't we give the info to Bernie and let him chase down Penrod. I'm missing the convention and my wife. If she hasn't divorced me yet," I said.

"Yeah, we have neglected our people. Let's go back to the hotel and talk to Bernie before he gives his speech." Doyle said.

Gus said. "I'll Call Bernie and warn him about Penrod."

We all stood and left the bar. I drove back to the hotel and we went into the ballroom. I called Penny, who said she and the women along with Oscar were in the restaurant having dinner. I realized I hadn't eaten, so I led Doyle and Gus to the restaurant. We had about an hour and a half before Bernie was going to speak.

"Have you solved the case yet?" Penny asked as I sat next to her.

"No, and I'm about fed up with it. I think I may go into another line of work. Do you need a personal assistant?"

"No, I manage well enough by myself. You could become a security guard on Buck's team. Sit around all night, sleep on the job. It's perfect for you."

"Funny. You should have a comedy show. About a woman who interviews celebrities. Or a reality show, about a woman who interviews celebrities and annoys her husband."

"Who will play the husband? George Clooney, maybe?"

"What is it with you and George Clooney?" I asked.

"He wouldn't be running off to fight crime."

"No, but he would be running off to make a movie."

"I could deal with that," Penny replied with a sly smile.

**

Chapter 22

We enjoyed our feast and then went back to the ballroom. It was crowded and noisy, two things I detested. We went to the front where the stage was set up and saw Bernie talking to one of the convention organizers. We waited until they were finished and Bernie noticed us, coming over.

"Thanks for the info on Penrod. It seems he's out of town, or so his aides say. Convenient for him. I'm having his financials and background looked into again. He's running for public office so he has to be squeaky clean," Bernie said.

Gus told Bernie what Mallone told us, in detail now. Bernie was quietly nodding as Gus elaborated. "That all could explain this mess and why Klein and Day were murdered. You were guessing it was Penrod?"

"It made sense, according to the feeling we got from Mallone," I said. "He stands to gain by blackmailing Saretta. Unfortunately for Penrod, the police have the photos now. So they don't do him much good."

"The photos are in evidence and won't be released unless there's a trial. Penrod could bring up the fact that Saretta had an affair with a hooker who was later murdered. It could still louse up Saretta."

"I would think Saretta could put a hit on Penrod," Gus said.

"He could, but that would make him the number one suspect. A murder charge would put a stop to his political career real fast," Doyle said.

"So, Penrod wins either way. Murder a few people and blame Saretta or catch Saretta having sex with a hooker," I said.

"I assume that would be his plan," Bernie said. "As soon as my men dig into him, we'll know something. Now I have to go get ready to talk to all you fine investigators."

Bernie went behind the stage and we went to our table. The chairman of the convention took the podium and called for attention. "Due to pressing city business, the mayor of Detroit couldn't be here last night to welcome us. But he's here tonight so please put your hands together to welcome him." The mayor stepped up from the back of the stage and went to the microphone.

He was getting ready to speak when someone in the room yelled out, "Where's Doyle?" Those who knew the story of the shooting of the mayor by Doyle, laughed.

The mayor grinned and said, "Mr. Doyle and I are on good terms now and I hope he doesn't shoot me again," he said with a good-natured laugh.

I looked at Doyle and he had an uneasy smile. I'm sure he'd like everyone to forget the incident. The mayor spoke for about five minutes, or four minutes too long, and managed to put a plug in for the upcoming elections. He thanked everyone and turned the mic over to Bernie as he stood next to the mayor.

"Let's all show our appreciation to the mayor for appearing," Bernie said into the mic. The crowd gave him a modest amount of applause as he waved and left the stage. Bernie cleared his throat, took out his notes and said,

"I'm Detroit Police Homicide Detective Bernie Longmire, and I'm not used to giving public speeches, but I'll try. Every investigator here knows that it's important to keep on the good side of local law enforcement. Just so you don't get arrested for messing up a crime scene."

That got a good reaction from everyone. Bernie went on talking about how we could coexist with law enforcement and cooperate.

"It's easy to be nice to your fellow police detectives, all working hard to bring criminals to justice. Most of you will be involved in following cheating spouses and never see a murder case. Doesn't mean it won't happen, but be assured the police won't invite you into their murder cases. If you get hired by a relative or friend of a murder victim, you can do your investigation, but remember the police have the first priority over your case. You are obligated to share information on anything you find out. Besides, it helps relationships between you and the officers, goodwill that goes a long way."

He spoke for about forty minutes, then took questions. It all went nicely, then he thanked everyone and turned the podium back to the chairman.

"Thank you Detective Longmire. We have a good line-up of lecturers all day tomorrow, then the closing ceremony tomorrow night. Okay, the bars are opening, so don't get too drunk, please," he said and walked off the stage.

Bernie found his way around to our table and sat. Gus leaned across the table and said, "Not bad, Bernie. You did good."

"I'm glad I didn't drink anything before talking. I might have peed my pants," Bernie replied. He took out his cell phone and turned it on, read the messages and stood. "I have to answer my messages." He turned away and went out of the room.

"I wonder if anything will come up on Penrod before I go back to Vegas?" I said.

"We'll keep you informed if we find out anything," Doyle said.

"I hope so," Penny said. "I'm not staying over in Detroit."

"I don't plan on staying either. So, even if this isn't solved, we'll be heading home Monday morning," I answered her.

We got our drinks from the bar and were sitting when Bernie returned. "What's up?" Gus asked.

"Got lots to tell," he said, taking a sip of his beer before speaking. "First, there were no reports of Penrod leaving the country as reported by his people. His finances showed that he took out ten thousand dollars from his business account, reason unknown. But three murders could be covered by that. Lastly, and this is the fun part, Penrod was involved this afternoon in a fender-bender up on Gratiot Avenue, north of Eight Mile. I guess he didn't make it out of the country. He's in holding for intoxication."

"Not a good way to start a political campaign," Doyle said.

"Now the best part," Bernie said and paused to take a drink of his beer. We waited while he set the can down and smiled. "Saretta's wife, Loretta, was in Penrod's car when he blew through a red light and swiped a van. There was a patrol car on the corner and the officer saw the whole incident. Loretta is being held for drunkenness and fighting with the officer. That should make Saretta real happy."

"Are you going to talk to Penrod?" I asked.

"I'll go in and question him. I don't have anything to tie him to the murders other than Mallone's statement," Bernie replied.

"Speaking of Mallone, did you get him set up with the Marshals?" Gus asked.

"He never showed up. Either he changed his mind or Saretta got to him. I had an officer going to check on him, but no word back yet."

"More bodies dropping," I said with a grin.

"It's possible. Now I have to finish my beer and go roust Penrod and see if I can get him to slip up and confess. At least we have Loretta Saretta in custody to help. Since she's drunk, she may spill the beans."

"Or her lunch," I said with a grin.

**

Chapter 23

Penny looked at me and said, "I suppose you're going to go watch Bernie interrogate this guy?"

"I have a moral obligation to follow this case through to the end," I replied.

"As long as it ends by tomorrow at midnight. We are out of here Monday morning."

"We'll be back in Vegas by Monday afternoon, so don't worry."

"We better be or I'll be talking to a divorce attorney," she threatened.

"You'd never divorce me, you're in my will."

"What? That pittance you plan to leave me? I would do better selling your ownership in the firm. Then I could travel and see the world."

Private Eye Murders

Buck called to me from his end of the table. "Jimmy, you do have the jet reserved for Monday morning?"

"Of course, Buck. It will be fueled and ready to fly." I thought it would be a good idea to call to make sure I did reserve the jet.

Bernie stood and said, "I'm going in to do some questioning before Penrod's lawyers screw it up. Anyone who cares to join me, better leave now." He turned and went out.

Doyle, Gus and I stood and said our goodbyes. Trapper said, "Nice of you to visit with us, Jim. Will you be on the jet going back?"

I gave him the finger and left. We went to my car again and drove to Bernie's precinct, the same place where Penny and her gang of criminals had been held. I had never spent much time in Detroit, most of my cases when I lived here involved the area north of the city. Doyle and Gus were native Detroiters so I had to follow their lead.

We arrived and went in. There were a number of people who knew Doyle from when he was on the force, his reputation preceded him.

We found Bernie talking to a uniformed officer, he waved to us as we stood waiting. He said something to the officer and then came to us.

"Penrod is in one of the interrogation rooms, and he's not happy," Bernie said.

"What if he lawyers up?" I asked.

"Then I'll threaten him with slipping the info of his arrest to the media. Along with having the wife of a competitor in the race for city council in his car. That would be embarrassing enough to make him talk."

"But not enough to make him confess to conspiracy to commit murder," Gus said.

"True, but I may get him to say something I can use. Besides, we still have Loretta to badger."

"She's a good actress from when we first met her," I said.

"Yeah, she had us believing her, until she pulled the gun," Doyle said.

"Well, we found a gun in her purse and I'm having ballistics check it against the bullets that killed Day and Klein. I'm sure it wasn't the gun used, but we'll have it on record. I'm going to talk to Penrod now." He turned and we followed. He pointed to the observation door and went in the room where Penrod sat fuming.

"I demand to be let out of here. You have no reason to hold me!" he yelled. Bernie sat across from him and smiled.

"Drunk while driving, good enough to hold you overnight. I can make you disappear in the system so you won't be out of here by Monday morning."

"I'm friends with the mayor and most of the city council. They'll have your badge."

"I'm sure they don't want to be associated with a drunk driver who was with the wife of his competitor for the council seat. They don't need the scandal."

Penrod sat back and said nothing. Bernie continued, "What do you know about the photos of Saretta?"

"I know nothing about them," he replied tersely.

"That's not what Loretta said," Bernie lied. "She admitted that she told you all about the private investigator she hired to catch her husband committing a crime."

"That bitch lied. She never told me about the photos of Saretta and the hooker."

"What hooker? I never said anything about a hooker."

"I want my lawyer."

"And I'll be talking to the media about your charges of drunk driving involving an accident."

I could see through the mirror glass that Penrod was getting red-faced. Not from embarrassment, but anger. He sat back and didn't say anything.

"I have nothing more to say," he finally spoke.

Bernie stood and went to the door and came out. We joined him in the hallway as he moved down to the room where Loretta was being held. He pointed to our door and we went in. Loretta had her head on the table, looking like she may have passed out. Bernie entered and she brought her head up, looking very much wiped out.

"Rough day, Mrs. Saretta?" Bernie asked.

"Screw you, cop," she spit back.

"Now, that's not nice, I'm trying to be friendly. Especially since Harvey Penrod has hinted that you had something to do with the murders of the private detective you hired."

Her eyes went wide and she yelled, "That rat bastard! I had nothing to do with any murders. Harvey engineered that."

"Why don't you tell me your side of the story? Maybe he lied and you can keep yourself out of the murders."

"You better believe it. I had nothing to do with the murders. I was having an affair with Harvey, and I told him I was going to have a P.I follow my husband. That's when Harvey brought up that thug hitman from Toledo to recover the photos. Klein called me as to where he hid the photos and I didn't know how to reach the hitman. So I went to the hotel to retrieve the photos, when I ran into the three little pigs."

I looked at Doyle and Gus and said, "Are we three little pigs?" They laughed.

"The hitman was screwing up everything by killing off Klein and then Day. Day was hired by my husband to find the photos. Lou found out from the hooker, who was working with Klein, that I hired Klein to get the goods on Lou. She came from Toledo with Klein to set up my husband for the sex. You want another laugh? Lou killed the hooker, to get her to talk. She didn't know where the photos were, so he hired Day. The hitman killed Day thinking he had the photos. It's a real mess."

"Just so Penrod doesn't get the jump on your information, why don't you write down everything you told me," Bernie said and pushed the pad to her.

She grabbed the pen and said, "Better believe I'll fry those bastards, both of them, Penrod and my husband."

Bernie smiled at the mirror and sat back watching her write furiously. Fifteen minutes later he gathered the pad and stood. He thanked Loretta and left her alone in the room. He came around to us and went to shut off the recording equipment that took down everything she said.

"I think that secures Penrod as the main suspect. Lou Saretta will have to answer a number of questions also. But I think the mess is pretty much wrapped up," Bernie said. "I'll get Saretta in and we'll have to get his statement."

"We still need to find the hitman," I said.

**

Chapter 24

"And here I thought we had this all sewn up," Doyle said. "The hitman is probably heading back to Toledo by now. He's the Toledo PD's problem."

"But they'll have to ship him back here for the murders he committed in Detroit," Bernie added.

"You're just as bad as Jim," Doyle said. "I wanted to enjoy the convention knowing we solved the murders and why. Now we have to find the hitman."

"We at least know it was both Penrod and Saretta who set up the hits. The hitman is just extra baggage," I said.

Bernie turned when he saw Saretta coming in with officers following. "They couldn't have found him that fast," Gus said.

"You!" Saretta said pointing at Bernie. "Are you the SOB who arrested my wife again?"

Bernie grinned, knowing Saretta came in voluntarily. He looked at us and said, "This makes it so much easier." He waited until Saretta moved close and said, "I have to advise you of your rights, Mr. Saretta." He read the Miranda rights to Saretta, as the man was protesting. "Do you understand your rights, Saretta?"

"What the hell are you talking about? I came to get my wife out of jail. Where is she?"

"You'll see her soon enough, but first I need to talk to you." Bernie motioned to the officers standing behind Saretta and said to take him to interrogations.

"Interrogations? What are you talking about?" Saretta yelled.

"We need to talk to you about your wife, Lou," Bernie said.

Saretta shut up and followed the officers. Bernie looked to us and said, "Here we go again."

We were back in observation as Bernie entered the other room. He sat across from Saretta and smiled.

"What are you smiling about, Chief Run-a-muck?" Saretta said.

Bernie lost his smile and said, "I was going to be nice about this, but since you are going to be a dickhead, I'm arresting you for the possible murder of Corletta Kemper."

"What!" He yelled. "I never killed her. She was alive when I left her."

"They found her dead in the motel room that you and she shared. According to your wife's testimony," he held up the pad, "you killed her when you found out she was helping to get photos of you and her. Then you sent Mike Day to retrieve the photos."

Saretta sat back, "And you are going to believe that lying little whore of a wife? She wanted to divorce me and tried to use the photos as proof that I was unfaithful."

"Which you were," Bernie said. "We checked on Day, he was a P.I. from Detroit, his wife said you hired him. We believe that Day was murdered by a hitman hired by your buddy, Harvey Penrod."

"Penrod! That bastard was trying to discredit me every chance he could. I found out from the hooker that she was hired to get photos on me. That bastard Klein had wireless cameras around the room and he was in a vehicle safely away from us collecting images. I left the hooker alive when I went after Klein. I didn't find him. So I hired Day to find him and the photos. That's all I have to say, get my lawyer."

Bernie stood and said, "That's all I needed to know, thank you Mr. Saretta." He turned and went out of the room.

"The plot thickens," Doyle said as Bernie came into observation shutting off the recording equipment.

"Yep, I'll get with the D.A. and give him all this. They can decide what to do with them now."

"Looks like there's an open seat for city council," Gus said with a grin.

"True, Gus. I'm tired and we have the main conspirators in custody," Bernie said. "Let's call this a night and go back to the convention while there's still time. I need a beer."

"Hopefully, the hitman is also finished for the night," I said.

We went back to my car and drove out, followed by Bernie in his car. The convention was still going in full force and we found Buck, Earl, Trapper, and Deacon having a good time at the table.

"Where are Lacey, Mac and the women?" I asked Buck.

"Oscar took them to the night club upstairs." Buck replied.

"Who has Jessie?" I asked.

"Penny. She went back to the room to relax, she said."

"Good, then I won't have to bail her out," I said.

Doyle, Gus and I went to the bar and got our beers, then back to the table. Bernie came in and went to the bar, got his drink and came over to us.

"So, are you good with what was found so far?" I asked Bernie.

"It's good, and explains a lot. I think we can get convictions based on the statements. I'll know more in the morning after the D.A. goes over the case."

We were enjoying the ambiance of the room and everyone in it. The private investigators were all whooping it up. I turned and saw Poppy, Marge and Oscar coming into the room. Poppy snuck up on Doyle and put her hands over his eyes from the back.

"Oh, Cathy, your hands are so warm," Doyle said. Poppy hit him on the back of the head.

"Screw you," Poppy said, sitting next to him.

"Well, you shouldn't sneak up behind me," Doyle replied.

"How was the club?" I asked.

Marge said, "It was boring. The music sucked and there weren't a lot of people having fun."

Poppy said, "We left before we could get into a fight. This place is dangerous, so much hostility. I guess when the drinks flow, people get stupid. How did you do on your killer?"

"We got two bad guys, who weren't smart enough to commit the perfect crime.

Unfortunately, there's still a hitman out there who needs to be taken down."

"And you don't know who he is?" Poppy asked.

"Not at all," Doyle replied. "Bernie, isn't there a data base of hitmen in Toledo?"

"I have my men checking the criminal scene down there. Hopefully we can identify one," he said.

"Marge, did you get to the lecture for office workers?" I asked her.

"I did, it was very useful. Lots of good ideas. Lacey and I sat through it and we did a lot of shop talk," Marge said.

"Where are Lacey and Mac?" I asked.

"They met some friends who came from Vegas."

"There are other investigators here from Vegas?" I asked.

"A couple, and Lacey said they were trying to talk her into joining their firm."

I thought about that and wondered if Lacey would leave us. "I hope she doesn't change jobs."

"She said she was perfectly happy where she was," Marge replied.

"I'm glad to hear that," I said.

Doyle looked across the table behind Buck and Deacon and groaned, "Oh, man."

"What?" Poppy asked him.

"You don't want to know," he replied.

A long-haired, blond woman, about forty, well-built and beautiful was standing behind Buck. She came around the table straight to Doyle and pulled his head back in his chair, planting a big kiss on his lips. Poppy sat waiting for an excuse from Doyle as the woman released him.

"Uh, um…hi Stoney," he said to the woman as he turned in his chair to her.

She grinned and said, "Hi, lover, how's tricks?"

**

Chapter 25

"Are you here for the convention?" Doyle asked nervously, glancing at Poppy. She sat with no expression, which Doyle took as a bad sign. He had a feeling it was going to be a cold night tonight.

"Well, there's that and I was hired to find a killer," she said bluntly.

"What killer?" Doyle asked.

"The murderer of Mike Day. I was hired by his wife to find the guy who did it. I hear you and your little playmates are looking for him also. Any luck?"

"None yet," Doyle said with a slight whimper, feeling Poppy's eyes penetrating his head. He turned and said, "Stoney, this is my girlfriend, Poppy Drake. Poppy, this is Stoney Hawk, an old friend."

"Is that all you think of me, lover? As an old friend? I'm hurt," the woman said, looking at Poppy. "I would keep a close eye on this one. I tried to get him to marry me years back but he was still too hung up on his late wife. Maybe you'll have better luck."

"No, I'm not interested in marriage," Poppy replied, frowning. "Especially with Doyle."

"Good girl, don't rush it. So Artie, what about the killer? Any leads yet?"

"We have four investigators working the case and nothing yet. We did find the suspect who hired the killer who murdered Day. He's in custody," Doyle said. "We have statements that he hired a hitman from out of Toledo, the hitman was the one who killed Day and Klein."

"That's a start. Well, I'll leave you people to your party. I have my people at another table. Good to meet you Poppy, hold on to him if you can, he's a keeper," Stoney said and went off laughing.

Doyle looked at Poppy and said, "It was years ago. She's a memory now."

Poppy picked up a napkin and wiped the lipstick off Doyle's mouth. "She better be a memory," she growled.

I said, "It must be nice to have women like that in your memory."

"Thanks Jim, don't mention it," Doyle said. I took the hint.

"So where do you know Stoney from?" Bernie asked.

"When I was in homicide, she was involved in an investigation about dangerous illegal drugs being sold to high school kids resulting in a couple of deaths. One of the parents hired her to find the dealers. She's a private investigator with her own firm. I met her when she came to my precinct, trying to get information from me."

"I'll bet she didn't have to try too hard," Poppy muttered. Doyle didn't respond.

"I know her from her reputation. Never met her, too bad it took so long," Bernie said, grinning at Doyle's discomfort. "I hear she's a tough woman to deal with, takes no prisoners."

"Yeah, she's no cream puff, she can be very dangerous. Even with my training on the FBI terrorist tactical team, I'd say she could do well on the team. She's trained in various martial arts and good at Krav Maga. I've seen her take down four men in an alley. Yes, she's dangerous."

"How did she get the name Stoney? Is it a nickname?" I asked.

"No, it's her real name. Her mother loved the song 'Stoney End' sung by Barbra Streisand back in 1971, and written by Laura Nyro, a year before Stoney was born, the name became hers."

"You're just a wealth of information about her, aren't you?" Poppy said.

"Hey, we were romantically involved. Not my first and not my last," Doyle said, bluntly now.

"I better be your last," Poppy warned.

"Yes, you are," he replied carefully. I was sure he was trying not to think about all the women he had been involved with.

I stood and said, "I think I'll go up to my room and see what Penny is up to." I said my goodbyes and left the ballroom. In the lobby I saw Stoney talking to a man. He looked like a cop, judging by his suit. She may have been trying to get information on the suspects in custody. I stood waiting for the elevator, when she came over.

"You're Jim Richards, correct?" she said with a lilt in her voice.

"I am, and you are Doyle's former flame," I replied.

She laughed and said, "Yes we had a fiery relationship. Who's the woman he's with now?"

"I only just met her and Doyle the other day. So I don't know much about them. I do know she's an investigator for an insurance company. You have an agency in Detroit?"
"Yes, but I'm moving it to Sterling Heights. I've been in Detroit for a long while, but the city is getting too busy for me."

193

Private Eye Murders

I was carefully checking her out, in her skin-tight black jumpsuit, low cut in the cleavage area. She was well-developed and athletic and had a mane of blond hair down to her waist.

"How do you manage all that hair?" I asked before thinking.

She laughed and said, "It's a wig. I wear it for social events, like this convention. It confuses people when I'm not actually working. My blond hair is shorter under the wig."

"Ah, like disguises," I said.

"I like to remain an enigma, and changing my looks helps. I also do a great bag lady," she smiled.

The elevator door finally opened and there stood Penny. She moved out and over to me.

I hoped talking to a great looking woman wouldn't give Penny reasons to question me. "Where's Jessie?" I asked, diverting the subject.

"Lacey and Mac came to get her and go back to their room to rest." Penny turned to the woman and said, "Hello, Stoney, good to see you again."

That took me by surprise.

"You too, Penny. Are you and Jim still married?" Stoney asked.

Penny looked at me and said, "For now, we are. You aren't thinking of stealing him from me are you, Stoney?"

"I don't fool around with married men, which is why I asked. Jim is someone who I would be interested in."

I could feel my ears burning, and cleared my throat.

"Well, you'd have to fight me for him, even though I know you would win." The two women laughed and Penny said to me, "Are you done with our friends in the convention?"

"I was just going up to see how you were doing. How do you know Stoney?"

"She was on one of my shows when I was here in Detroit, to give examples to women on how to protect themselves from attackers. A good show, by the way," she said to Stoney.

"Thanks, I enjoyed it. Well, I'll leave you two to enjoy the fest. I have work to do." She smiled at me and went off.

"Did I interrupt something?" Penny asked poking me in the ribs.

"No, my dear, we were just talking about Doyle and Poppy. It seems Stoney was romantically involved with Doyle a number of years ago. There was a bit of tension when Stoney came over and gave Doyle a big kiss. I think Poppy was ready to do something."

"I don't blame her," Penny said watching Stoney walk away. "Nice ass," Penny said.

"Hey, you'd kill me if I said that," I complained.

"But you were thinking it, weren't you."

"Me, never," I said, involuntarily glancing at Stoney. Penny whacked me and walked toward the ballroom.

**

Chapter 26

We re-joined our friends and associates at the table. I went to get a couple beers for Penny and myself, then saw Gus talking to Bernie by the entrance to the ballroom. They said a few words and Bernie went out. I caught up to Gus as he was heading back to the table.

"Bernie leaving?" I asked.

"Yeah," Gus said, stopping. "He has paperwork to finish for the D.A. tomorrow so he can get Penrod and Saretta up before a judge."

We continued to the table. "I'm glad we found a number of clues to help Bernie get this all together."

"I'd say from what Bernie tells me, it's over and we just have to find the hitman now."

"Does Bernie think he's still in Detroit or gone back to Toledo?"

"Bernie never really talks much about his feelings on a case. He's a quiet sort of person. His Native-American heritage has a lot to do with that."

"He seems to be a calm type," I said. "Does he ever get mad?"

"I've seen him blow off a number of times. I wouldn't want to be on his bad side if he ever really got mad."

We arrived at the table and I handed Penny her beer. She and Poppy had their heads together talking. Probably about Stoney. It was good that Penny knew Stoney so she could answer questions that Poppy may have had.

I sat watching Earl, Buck and Trapper going over the brochures they collected from the vendors. I figured tomorrow they'd spend their limit bringing back gadgets to our firm. That was fine with me. I saw a few things that I'd like to have.

Doyle was talking to Marge, then he leaned to me and said, "What did you think of Stoney?"

I grinned and said, "Turns out Penny knew her from years ago. I was lucky when Penny caught us talking in the lobby."

"What was Stoney saying?"

"Nothing about you, mostly wondering what we had on the hitman. She did tell Penny that if we weren't married, she'd be interested in me," I said with a bigger grin.

"Stoney is hot for a lot of men. That girl couldn't get enough when we were together." Doyle shut up when he saw Poppy looking at him. She was too far away to hear and the room was noisy, so he was safe.

I noticed Gus took out his cell phone after it started ringing. He answered, listened and then hung up. He leaned to Doyle and me and said, "Small problem. Seems Penrod never finished paying the hitman off for his work. They released Mrs. Saretta and Bernie got a call that she was taken by the hitman. He said Bernie was to release Penrod so he could pay his debt, or Loretta would go for a swim in the river."

"This is getting good. Not for Loretta, but for our case. Did the hitman say where he was to get the cash?" I asked.

"An exchange would be arranged by the hitman, after Penrod is free to go," Gus said.

"Has Bernie let Penrod out?" Doyle asked.

"Yep, about ten minutes ago. He has men following him, but it may not help. Bernie put a tap on Penrod's cell phone, so he could find out what is going to go down. The hitman isn't stupid, he won't come out in the open, so the exchange is going to be covert."

"Is there anything we can do?" Doyle asked.

"I think Bernie was hoping that we'd get involved," Gus said. "He trusts us enough to help get this under control. Penrod told the hitman on his cell that he would have to go back to his office to get the money from his safe. So we could start there."

"Let's go, time is wasting," I said and told Penny that crime was afoot. She gave me her usual sigh and said to go.

I asked Gus if he knew where Penrod's office was, he said he did. We got in my car again and I followed Gus' directions. It was an office building down on Michigan Avenue. Doyle said it was close to his office.

We parked across the street and watched the building. There were lights on in a couple lower offices and we could see movement. There was only one main entrance to the building through a lobby, so we could see most of the first level.

"There's Penrod," Gus said as a man came out of a door along the lobby hallway. We watched him go to the entrance and walk out to Michigan Avenue. He had a car parked at the curb and got in. We followed him over to Woodward and then south.

"I wonder if Bernie knows where he's going?" I said.

"I'm amazed that Penrod is so concerned for Loretta's safety that he'd do this," Gus said.

"She must have been very good to him in bed. He's acting like a fool for her," Doyle spoke.

Private Eye Murders

"Where are Bernie's men who were supposed to be following him?" Gus asked.

"They're right behind us," I said. "They've been following since we left Penrod's office. I'm surprised Bernie is letting us get involved in this."

"Actually, Bernie never said for us to follow him. I just assumed it," Gus admitted.

"I'm sure he figured we would," I said. "Now where's he going?" I said as Penrod pulled around the Cobo Hall drive.

"Damn, is he going to the boat docks where I shot the mayor? I don't need a repeat of this," Doyle moaned.

We stopped just outside the parking area and watched Penrod drive in toward the boat dock. He stopped and waited. The car following us pulled up next to us and I could see Bernie in the front seat. He grinned and then watched Penrod.

Another car pulled into the parking lot from a different road and over to Penrod's car. It stopped and a man got out. Penrod exited his car and stood, holding a small bag.

We could hear Penrod yell, "Where's Loretta?"

The man went to his trunk and opened it, pulling the woman up and out. She was tied and gagged by duct tape. The man walked her around to the front of his car and said something to Penrod. We couldn't hear him. Penrod held the bag out and gave it to the man. He opened the bag and looked in, then pushed Loretta towards Penrod.

The hitman pulled a gun and shot Loretta, then Penrod. Bernie was yelling to go. His car and ours drove out to them. The hitman was already in his car driving down the road going away from us. Bernie was pursuing the hitman as I drove to Penrod and Loretta. We got out as I heard a loud crash coming from where the other cars were heading.

Gus went to the two people on the ground and said, "Penrod and Loretta are still alive, but weak." He pulled out his cell phone and called for help. I was watching the area where the other cars went. I called to Doyle to come with me, and told Gus to stay with the victims.

I drove towards the road they took, which was going towards Hart Plaza and saw three cars, two had plowed into each other. Bernie and his men from the other car were going through the wreck pulling the hitman out. I saw a figure standing by the other car, it looked like a woman.

"Stoney," Doyle said as we pulled up and got out.

**

Chapter 27

We went over to the wreck as Stoney moved close to us. "What happened?" I asked her.

"My source in the precinct said they were releasing Penrod to pay the hitman. I heard the woman was involved. I followed the police car, and your car, but when you parked where you did, I went around to this entrance of the parking lot and waited. I watched the hitman shoot the couple and then he drove my way. I decided to stop him the best way I could, I rammed him." She looked at her car with its front end caved in.

I was laughing and said, "It was one good way to stop him. Good thing you weren't hurt."

"I jumped out just before the cars collided," she said,

I looked back to see Bernie and the cops had the hitman sitting on the ground, looking dazed. "Well, he's out of business now. There were plenty of witnesses who saw him shoot Penrod and Loretta."

Bernie came over as his men were taking the hitman to a patrol car that just arrived. "Stoney, thank you for saving us a mad car chase through Detroit," he said to her.

"My pleasure. Now I can tell Day's wife I stopped the hitman who killed her husband."

"I pulled his wallet and his name is Walter Jefferson. We now have a name finally. I was getting tired of everyone referring to him as the hitman."

Private Eye Murders

About an hour later, Penrod and Loretta had been taken by an EMS unit, and a wrecker was pulling the two damaged cars apart. Then they put them on a couple of flatbed tow trucks and hauled them away. Doyle and Stoney were sitting on the hood of my rental car. I was walking around watching all the activity and glad it was over. Now I could relax on the last day of the conference. Bernie and Gus came to us as I moved to the car.

"Stoney, I can get you a ride to wherever you want to go," Bernie told her.

"That was the company car I wrecked, it's insured. My personal car is at my office, if someone could take me there."

Bernie called to one of his officers and yelled for him to drive his car over. He did and Bernie said to take Stoney wherever she wanted to go. The young officer looked delighted to have Stoney in his car. Stoney said her goodbyes to us and left with the cop.

"Well, that brings this to a satisfying conclusion," Doyle said. He looked at his watch and said, "The party is still going on, shall we go celebrate?"

Gus, Doyle and I went to get in the car as Bernie went to his car. We drove back to the hotel and went in to the ballroom. There were still a good number of people enjoying the pleasure of the company of others. Penny, Poppy and Marge were nowhere to be seen. That worried me.

Buck grinned and said, "Penny said if you ever returned, to tell you they went clubbing. Think they'll get arrested again?"

"I hope not. Did Oscar go with them?" I asked.

"He did, although I think he wasn't happy about it," Buck said.

Doyle laughed and said, "I'm sure he's not fond of babysitting the women. I'll have to give him a bonus."

We sat around talking about the incident in the parking lot as the evening wore down. The women hadn't returned yet, but at two in the morning the bars closed all over town. It was now almost two. I stood, said I was going to my room and said I'd see everyone in the morning. I was going to the elevator when I saw Penny, Poppy, Marge and Oscar coming in the front entrance. They all looked a little inebriated. I laughed as Penny wavered walking over to me. The others went in the ballroom to find Doyle.

"I can't take you anywhere without you getting drunk," I said sternly.

"Hey, this is a special occasion. I never had this much fun with Lynn, she's too stiff," Penny slurred her words.

"I'll tell Lynn you said that. Now, we need to get you to bed."

"Hey, sailor, are you propositioning me?"

"Sure, let's get a room and make wild love."

We arrived at the room and went in. I went to let Willy out of the bathroom and when I turned, Penny was sprawled on the bed, snoring loudly. I slept on the couch that night with Willy after tucking her in bed.

Early the next morning, the last day of the convention, I called for room service to bring breakfast up to the room. I ordered for Penny, not knowing if she was going to eat. During the night I heard her in the bathroom a couple times, so I was sure her stomach was empty.

I felt sorry for my little girl. She had an interesting life, but never really cut loose like she had this weekend. She'd remember this for long time.

"Close the damn curtains," came a yell from the bedroom. I went in and over to the windows, pulling the curtains shut. "Thank you," she said weakly.

I sat on the edge of the bed and stroked her head. "I've never gotten this drunk. If I do it again, please shoot me."

I promised I would. "Are you going to be well enough to get up and go check out the convention? It is the last day."

"No, I'll lay here and suffer until I feel better. Go have your fun. Did you catch your killer?"

"As a matter of fact we did. Or I should say Stoney stopped him. He's in custody now and I'm done with the case."

Private Eye Murders

Willy was at my feet, I picked him up and put him on the bed. He went right for Penny's face and started to lick.

"Ah, no! Doggy kisses! Not now, Willy," she moaned.

I pulled him away and put him back on the floor. "He just feels bad for you," I said.

"Fine, ask him to send me a sympathy card. I want to be left alone for a while. I'll call you when I'm ready to walk among the living."

I kissed her forehead and took Willy out with me, closing the door.

The breakfasts came and I tipped the man. I was still at the open door when I saw Poppy. She smiled grimly and came over. "Aren't you on the wrong floor?" I asked.

"I just came to see if Penny was all right," she said, with a slight lisp.

"She's still sleeping. She's suffering badly. How are you and Marge?"

"It took all I had to come here. Marge is still in her bathroom, I think sleeping on the floor. I'll go back and drop dead. Doyle is up and getting ready to go out, so us women will have the rooms to ourselves." She turned and went back to the elevator. I closed the door and pushed the food cart to the table. I ate my breakfast and then ate Penny's also. Then I got ready to go out.

My cell phone buzzed and I answered, it was Doyle. "Are you ready to go explore the vendors one more time?" he said in my ear.

"I'll meet you in the lobby. I'm almost ready." I hung up and gathered my things, then put Willy in the bathroom. He wasn't happy.

**

Chapter 28

I walked into the lobby and found Doyle with Gus. "Well, gentlemen, what case shall we solve today?" I asked jokingly.

"The case of our missing girlfriends and wives," Doyle said back.

"That's no mystery. Is Oscar feeling no pain this morning?" I asked.

"Actually, he's feeling quite well. He's in the ballroom scouting out spy equipment for our office. Shall we go join him?"

We were going into the ballroom as I asked Gus, "Is Bernie joining us today?"

"Nope, he wants to get the case all signed, sealed and delivered to the D.A.'s office. He said he may join us later."

"Even on a Sunday, law enforcement never rests," I said as we walked down the rows of vendors, hawking their gadgets. I spent time at a few booths examining the toys they offered and placing orders at a few.

Doyle, Gus and I went to sit at a table to relax. There was a lecture going on about how to dig into a suspect's finances without involving the police. Which was illegal, but as private investigators we could skirt the issue.

I looked around and saw Lacey, Mac and Jessie coming in. I excused myself and went to them. "So did you enjoy the Detroit Zoo?" I asked.

Lacey said, "Yes, it was a lot of fun. Thanks for telling us about it."

Jessie held up a banner with lions on the flag. "Look, we saw the lions, they were really big," she beamed.

"Did you get to listen to any lectures about office procedures?" I asked Lacey.

"Yes, and the office is going to be run with an iron fist," she said with a grin. "Where's Penny?"

"She's a little under the weather, induced by spirits."

"Drunk?" Lacey said with a smile.

"No, hung over badly, though," I said.

"Did you get pictures?" Lacey said with a laugh.

"I didn't think about it. But if she's still in bed suffering, I will."

They went to get some lunch and I went back to Doyle and Gus. Buck, Earl and Trapper had joined them now and we all sat listening to the lectures.

Just after two, Penny, Poppy and Marge managed to make it out of their rooms and came over to where we were. I wasn't going to say anything; I knew she was still suffering. I'd been there a number of times in my life, and didn't need people reminding me.

We relaxed the rest of the day and caught a show in the showroom. They had a very funny comedy magician and we enjoyed him. We went back to the ballroom and they had two more lecturers so we listened, then they had a closing ceremony, which was nice.

The bars opened for the evening and we all sat around bragging about our weekend. It came and went so fast, it was all a blur. I saw Stoney talking to a few people and she waved to me. Penny was very quiet and not drinking, and I let her have her space.

I announced to my people that the jet would be ready to go by ten in the morning. So we had to be there early. They all agreed, I think they were missing Vegas. Detroit MGM Grand was interesting but it didn't have the vitality that Vegas did.

Just before the evening ended, I took Doyle and Gus aside and said, "It was a real pleasure working with the both of you. Look me up if you ever get to Vegas."

"Jim, your reputation is still intact with me," Doyle said. "It was fun, and I got to learn a few investigator tricks from the lectures. Not to mention Oscar loading up on gadgets for our cases."

Private Eye Murders

Gus smiled and said, "It was a good weekend, now back to chasing cheating spouses."

I looked behind Doyle and saw Stoney coming up behind him. She blew on his ear and he jumped. "Damn it, Stoney, you about gave me a heart attack," he said when he turned to see the woman grinning at him.

"Sorry, Artie, but it got your heart pumping, didn't it?" She kissed him on the cheek, "Glad to have met you, Jim and Gus. Maybe we'll work together on another case one day. I'd love to see Vegas, say hi to Penny for me." She gave me and Gus a kiss on the cheek, so we all had lipstick on our faces. She turned and vanished into the crowd.

"That's quite a woman," I said to Doyle.

"You don't know the half of it. She actually frightened me when we worked together. She took chances that I would never have, but she got the job done," he paused then held out his hand. "I have to go gather my people and get some sleep. Maybe I'll see you in the morning before you leave town."

"I hope so," I replied.

He said his farewells to Gus and left us. "Are you staying the night?" I asked Gus.

"I paid for it, may as well enjoy it. I have a daughter and a dog waiting for me at home in the morning. Good to meet you Jim. Keep in touch." We shook hands and he went off.

I stood alone in the crowd of investigators, when I felt a hand on my shoulder. It was Penny.

"I'm not feeling like being a pest to you tonight and I'm definitely not going out to a club. I just want to sleep my last night here and go back home."

"I'll wake you bright and early to get ready." We went up to our room and I knocked on Lacey's door. She answered and asked if I was ready to go home. "I am. Are you guys ready to go?"

"We just finished packing and will be ready in the morning." I left her and went into my room for the night.

Around seven-thirty the next morning I put our bags in the hallway for the porter to come get them. Everyone else was up and ready.

"I called the jet service to make sure they had breakfast on the flight for us," I told everyone in the hall. "So as soon as the bags are loaded and in the van, we can depart the hotel."

I watched the hotel disappear as we drove out to the airport. It just wasn't Vegas. We got to the airport, our bags were loaded on the jet and we were in our seats. Jessie was holding Willy and he was giving her his kisses as she giggled.

The ground dropped quickly as the jet ascended and we were on our way. I looked out the window to barely see Detroit in the distance and thought about what new adventures would be coming our way back home. As Dorothy said, "There's no place like home" and my favorite quote was the old saying, "Once you live in Vegas and get sand in your shoes, you may leave, but you always come back." And we were going back.

THE END

If you enjoyed reading about Stoney, here's the first chapter from her first book, "Stoney Hawk" coming soon.

Chapter 1

"I was born from love and my poor mother worked the mines
    I was raised on the good book Jesus
    Till I read between the lines
    Now I don't believe, I want to see the whole morning."

The Barbra Streisand song, "*Stoney End*" played on my car radio and I thought of my mother. She never worked the mines, but her job working in a laundry of a hotel, was just as bad. I was born in 1972 from a quickie union between a man and my mother. My father left before he even knew about my mother's pregnancy and all these years I wondered who he was. My mother refused to say, so I pretended that he was some big name rock star my mother met with in the band's bus after his show.

Private Eye Murders

My mother loved this song so when I was born, I became Stoney. I was glad her favorite song wasn't *'Jeremiah Was a Bullfrog.'* She died two years ago and still refused to tell me who my father was. I reached over and spun the volume dial to ear-bleeding loud and sang along.

I think the biggest reason I got into private investigating was because I wanted to solve the mystery of who my old man was. My real name was Stoney Iskowitz, but luckily my mother married and I took his last name, Hawk. I liked the sound of Stoney Hawk, it sounded tough and dangerous, which is what I trained myself to be. I grew up in a bad area of Detroit, a place where you fought almost every day to survive. As a girl growing up there, I fought the best of the punks who inhabited the neighborhood and after a while they left me alone.

After high school, having a reputation for being the bad girl, I joined the Army. I went through basic training and took the taunts and threats from the other maggots. After basic I was assigned a desk job in the headquarters of the Army Special Forces. I would watch the men training and made a few friends who took me in and taught me their expertise in combat and black ops. I left the Army when my time ended and went on a quest to find my father.

I found out from an old P.I. in Detroit that I could get more information by having a license to investigate. So I went to a local community college and took the classes and eventually got my license. I was now officially a private investigator.

I went to work for a while on my own and still had no luck finding anything about my father. My mother never kept records or a diary about her life. The father's name part of my birth certificate was left blank, so was my heart. I gave up looking and concentrated on my new profession. I took numerous classes in martial arts and Krav Maga.

I would hit the gym and work out, being hit on by a number of pumped up numbskulls. I never married, although I had one brush with a cop named Doyle. We lasted for about a half year, but he wasn't interested in marriage. He lost his wife in a car accident and couldn't let go of her memory. I left him and struck out to work my profession and got busy fairly fast.

Private Eye Murders

I drove out to Eastpointe to where I was to meet with a new client. She was having problems with her ex and wanted him out of her life. I was doing protection occasionally and equalizing problem cases. I usually could convince a trouble making ex-spouse or misguided boyfriend to back off.

I drove into the parking lot of the restaurant at Gratiot and Nine Mile Road. I didn't know what she looked like, but I had described myself. Curly blond hair down to my waist and tall. I always wore a spandex jumpsuit, it was easy to move in when I had to move fast. I may have looked like a hooker most of the times, but it was useful the rest of the times.

I entered the place and saw a woman alone in a booth waving to me. I went to her and sat.

"Marcy?" I asked. She said she was. "I'm Stoney Hawk, what can I do for you?" I knew what she wanted, but I wanted her to say the words aloud.

"My ex is bothering me, threatening me. I want him gone. The police can't do anything, I'd have to be beaten to a pulp before they could stop him and it would be only temporary. I'm afraid to even leave my house." She looked on the verge of tears.

"Did you bring the photo I asked for?"

She nodded her head and took a photo out of an envelope and handed it to me. "His name is Brian Estes."

I looked at the man and said, "This is a good shot. Thanks."

"What's your fee, Miss Hawk?"

"For domestic violence cases, I charge nothing. I'm just glad to make the world a little safer from the scum. When was the last time you saw him?"

"Late last night, he was out front of my house honking his horn. Then he spray painted my garage door, it said slut." Now she started crying softly.

"Has he ever beaten you?"

"Yes, a number of times. I ended up in the hospital twice and the police still couldn't do much. He was arrested, but he was released the next day after posting a small bail."

"How often do you see him?"

"Almost every day now. He just won't quit."

"Well, I have some friends who may want to talk to him, so I'll take care of it. Give me a few days. If you see him, or me, out front of your house, just stay in."

"Thank you, Miss Hawk. I don't know where else to go. I'm glad I found your ad in the paper. It's good to know there are people who care."

"No problem, go home and rest. I'll call when this is settled," I said and stood. I left the restaurant and drove back to my office in Detroit. I was in the process of moving it to Sterling Heights, I had gotten tired of the city.

I went into the building and checked my phone messages. Nothing of importance, so I sat and thought about my ad. I grew up watching an 80's TV show called the Equalizer, with British actor Edward Woodward. I loved watching him solve people's problems the same way I would handle Brian Estes. His name was Robert McCall, an unaffiliated private eye, and he always put an ad in the paper for his services. He worked outside of the law, but never did anything illegal. Well, most of the time. I didn't like the movie remake with Denzel, it just wasn't right to use the original idea and twist it around. Of course, they made it updated and modern, but it just wasn't the original.

I picked up my desk phone and placed a call. I waited until someone answered. "May I talk to Special Agent Maxwell?" I asked. I waited until Maxwell came on. "Larry, this is Stoney. I have a new case."

**

Continued in the book.

'Stoney End' from The Essential Barbra Streisand 1971
Songwriter, Laura Nyro
Lyrics Published by © Sony/ATV Music Publishing LLC

~~*~~

More books by Bob Moats

The Fatal Series - Fatal Rejection * Fatal
Departure * Fatal Romance * Fatal Outbreak
* Fatal Abduction * Fatal Seance

Doyle, P.I. Series - Doyle's Law * Doyle's
Justice * Doyle's Quest * Doyle's Paradise *
Doyle's Haunting

Also Bob's first juvenile book, "Crystal
Prison of Kyr"

The Jim Richards books by Bob Moats

(In series order)
Classmate Murders
Vegas Showgirl Murders
Dominatrix Murders
Mistress Murders
Bridezilla Murders
Magic Murders
Strip Club Murders
Made-for-TV Murders
Mystery Cruise Murders
Talk Show Murders
Sin City Murders

Black Widow Murders
Vegas Vigilante Murders
Area 51 Murders
Mortuary Murders
Hypnotic Murders
Sunshine State Murders
Blue Suede Murders
Honky Tonk Murders
Dark Carnival Murders
Lipstick Murders
Pasta Murders
Talent Show Murders
Shyster Murders
Campground Murders
Network Murders
Reunion Murders
Big Apple Murders
Kennel Murders
Trick or Treat Murders
Santa Murders
Wiseguy Murders
Toxic Murders

For a preview or to purchase a book, go to
http://murdernovels.com

Jim Richards Family of Readers

Thanks to the following people who are now part of the Jim Richards Family of Readers. They have read a book or more and enjoyed them. They all volunteered to be included in the list. If you are a fan of the books, send me your full name, and you will be included in future books. Send your name to murdernovels@bobmoats.com to be added here and on the website.

* Achim Feifel * Al Norris * Alex Wheatley * Alexandra Delporte-Wilkinson * Amy Tapia * Andrea Bryan * Anne Shepherd * Arianda Sugar * Arlene Markowski * Ashley Augustus * Audra Hall * Barbara Hughes * Barbara Sammons * Barbara Schuler * Barbara Zirger * Beth Donohue Plenskofski * Beth Rosin * Betsy Childress * Beth Gibson * Bill Sandy * Bill Tornquist * Billie-jo Collie * Boni J Rychener * Candace Larson * Carl Bishopric * Carla Lewis * Carole Henderson * Carolyn Conroy * Carolyn Riddle-Linington * Cassy Bailey * Cathie

Turner * Chad Hudson * Charlie Meier * Charlotte L Duran * Cheryl L. Everett * Cindy Ackley Nunn * Cindy Valstad * Connie Bancroft * Corinne Kay O'Daniel * Carol Beier * Dana Robbins Chuchran * Dana Wichita * Daniel Kalus * Danielle Monique * Darren Heald * Dave Travers * David Wilkinson * David Wiman * DeAnn Jannereth * Deanna Miller * Deb Breuker Balbo * Debbie Carter * Debbie White * Deborah Fartuch * Deborah Gauze * Deborah Sullivan * Dee King * Denise Freeman * Diana Carver * Dianne Procopio * Dixie Beck * Donna Gould * Donna Thompson * Donny Minter * Doris Kight * Eddie Moore * Eric Walters * Felicia Annette Bradfield * Francine Menor * Gail Chesney * Georgiann Minster * George Conner * Greg Colucci * Hayley Rankin * Harold Garcia * Heidi Arnold * Herb Muir * Irma Ranee Coy * Jacqueline Moss * Jan Kimball * Jane Lawson * Janice Schneider * Janice Spoor * Jeanette Mulroy * Jennifer Redmond * Jerry Dornak * Jessica Keown-Belous * Jim Beck * Jo Boguslaw * Jo Turner * Joanne Marie Turner * John Peiffer * John Wisbiski * Joseph Wauro * Joyce Stacy * Joyce Trifiletti

Private Eye Murders

* Judy Franklin * Judy Travers * Judy Padgett * Julie Heath * Junnahvee Benson * Karen Dahl * Karen Grams * Karen Higham * Karen Kaiser * Karen Meinburg Richwine * Karen Kirkman Parker * Karin Hawkins * Karin Vasvari * Kathleen Donohue Roesing * Kathleen Riddle-Wolfe * Kathy Hinds Moore * Kathy Jones * Kathy Mitchell * Katie Benzler * Kay Burns * Kelly Garcia * Ken Boggs * Keota Rodriguez * Kiera Mccarthy * Kim Estes * Kimberley May * Kitty Stolle * Kristie Sciler * Kirsty Stanton * LaLonnie Scallen * Larry Morris * Leann Parr * Lenora Scales * Leslie Marie Jackson * Linda Forester * Linda Ingle Cox * Linda Kennerö * Linda Magill * Lisa Bower * Lisa Keller * Liz Gibson * Lorraine Wiman * Loretta Alexander * Lynda Bowles * Lynette Lawrance * LuAnn Louttit * Manny Rothman * Marcia Gibson DeWitt * Marie Calder * Marlene Bryan * MaryLouise Kramp * Mary Lynn Gross * Megan Atkins * Meghan Hyden * Melissa Wescoat * Melody Cannavan * Merri Taylor * Michael Carruthers * Michael Dinkens * Michael Vannoy * Michelle Burns-Mitchell * Michelle Pilcher * Micki Potter * Mike

Moats * Mikki Gregory * Mimi Baur * Myrna Hecht * Nadine Sutton * Nancy Ellen Sayre * Nancy Graveman Davis * Natalie Quine * Neena Martin * O'Della Wilson * Pat Pollington * Pat Rohn * Patricia Jarmon * Patricia C Trezza * Patrick Barry * Paul Lawrance * Peggy Davis * Phyllis Bassett * Raylene Matheny * Rebecca Collins Besner * Renee Brumley * Reta Hanna * Reta Moats * Robert Lenski * Roberta Meister * Roberta Navarro-Harder * Sally Berneathy * Sally Hubler * Sarah Santos * Satka Nikc * Sharon E. Edwards * Sharon Mangini * Sharon McMillon * Sheena Rawl * Sherry Amstutz * Shirley Alvarez * Shirley Davies * Shirley Williams * Stacie Rowe * Stephanie Conner * Steve Cullen * Susan Haughton * Susan Hesse Adams * Susan Salomon * Suzan K Chase * Taisha Cullum * Tamara Moore * Tammy Castleberry * Tammy Lynn Wood * Ted Murphy * Terri Atkins * Terri Creech * Terry Raab * Tonia Rachael Riggs-Williams * Tonya Mann * Travis Fleury-Lopez * Twyla Gawlas * Val Brooks * Walt Munsel * Yvonne Isakson *

Thank you to all these wonderful people.

Thank you for purchasing this book. I hope you enjoy it as much as I enjoyed writing it for my faithful readers. Please feel free to email me to tell me what you thought about my stories. I love hearing from the readers and I do reply. I can be reached at murdernovels@bobmoats.com

Thanks again!